About the author

Sue Woodcock was born in London and brought up by her grandmother in the home counties. She went to St Swithuns school at Winchester, and then on to technical college. She joined the Hampshire Constabulary where she served in many roles for nearly thirty years, ending as a country beat officer on a motorcycle. She then moved to Yorkshire, became a shepherd in the Dales and did many jobs. On retiring from that, she settled down in the Yorkshire Wolds, writes a weekly diary in the *Yorkshire Post*, sings in three choirs, and has three elderly dogs. She enjoys wool-craft, needlework, music, gardening, nature and some public speaking.

HIDDEN BELOW - A SAUL CATCHPOLE NOVEL

Sue Woodcock

HIDDEN BELOW - A SAUL CATCHPOLE
NOVEL

Vanguard Press

A CIP catalogue record for this title is
available from the British Library.

ISBN 978-1-80016-029-3

*Vanguard Press is an imprint of
Pegasus Elliot MacKenzie Publishers Ltd.*
www.pegasuspublishers.com

First Published in 2021

**Vanguard Press
Sheraton House Castle Park
Cambridge England**

Printed & Bound in Great Britain

Dedication

For my friends, especially Hilary Forde, for her
help, and to all our wonderful NHS staff and
emergency workers

Acknowledgements

With thanks to Rachel Thomson, for her cover artwork.

Dramatis Personae

Murder Squad

Detective Chief Superintendent Saul Catchpole
Detective Inspector Alan Withers
Detective sergeants: Geoff Bickerstaff, Paul Christie
Detective constables: Julia Pellow, Caroline
Tarik Singh, Malcolm Austin, Sean Hawkins,
Simon, Peter.
Police Constables: Sharon Wright, Simon Hart,
Marco Verdi.
Office managers: Fred Dunlop, Nita Patel,
Paddy O'Grady

Other Police Officers

Deputy Chief Constable Taylor
Superintendent Wally Evans (Complaints and
Discipline)
Inspectors: Pollock, Harmer
Sergeants: Peter Toller, Shields, Boniface,
DS Rankin
Constables: Tony Gilchrist, Les Pike, Tim Virgo,
Vince, Tim Mason, Oliver Cody, Matt Buse,
Mandy O'Dell, Mick Pantin, Helen Pickering,
Neville Brown, PC Martin, Alf
From Lancashire: Superintendent Keith, WDC
Cox

Deputy Chief Constable David Owen
(Northumberland Police)
Home office: DCC Spedding
Training department: Archie.
Force psychiatrist: Ashley

Woodyard staff
Robert (Bob) Moreby, Elizabeth Moreby, Darren,
Bill Birtwhistle

Travellers
Petunia (Mary Alison Letts), Reuben, (Derek Thomas),
Caleb and Mary Jones, their nephews, Aaron, Seth,
Cain
Other suspect: Robert Galliver, truck driver

Victims
The Stevens family: Arnold, Bettina, Jason
Darren Cole, Nathan Cox, Ruth and Mark Jones
Suspect
Robert Galliver (truck driver)
Others
Gladys, Sid, and Lydia, Sharon's neighbours
Perter Clark (truck driver)
Miles (dentist)
Mr Edwards (bank manager)
George (mortuary attendant)

Lorde Clarke (landowner)

Saul's family and friends
Anna (wife) and children: Stephen, Samuel, Susan,
Sharon
Grandson: Benjamin
Brother: Jake, sister-in-law Diana
Farmworkers: Nick, John

Animals
Cat: Mung
Dogs: Hercules, Boo (Flyte)

Chapter 1

Petunia waited patiently in the undergrowth at the end of the lane. She watched as the workers from the timber yard left in their cars. The boss was the last to go, in his four-wheel drive. He closed the gates and locked them, got into his car and drove away.

Petunia was not her real name; that was left behind long before. She called herself Petunia, mainly to get her social security benefits. She was a new age traveller, moving around the country, and she lived in a caravan with her partner, Reuben. His artwork brought in some money and they had made a reasonable sum at the Appleby Horse fair the previous week. She had sold most of her sculptures, which were mainly of horses and traditional Romany caravans. Reuben had sold all his pictures.

She had parked her van further up the lane, well out of sight. Nor was it wise for any nosy parkers spotting that the number plate was a wrong'un. She waited fifteen minutes after the boss had left and, armed with a large number of empty feed bags gathered from the deserted farm yard a few nights before, she went through the hole that had been cut in the chain link fence and walked into a deserted timber yard. She followed the main drive between huge stands of felled tree trunks. She knew where they kept the firewood. She had been several times before and had even paid once when a worker had been on site.

This time she had no intention of paying as the place was deserted. They didn't want the firewood anyway, she reasoned to herself. She found a small hand trolley hidden behind the massive climbing hydrangea that was in flower, that covered the old brick building that was used as an office.

Passing the huge machinery vehicles she pulled the trolley close to one of the huge timber storing barns. The firewood pile beside the barn was much bigger than usual. She opened a bag and began filling it with bits of wood that were a suitable size for her. She only wanted ones that would fit in her wood burning stove. She filled another bag with kindling from a smaller nearby pile. She knew that Rueben and the others from the camp would soon be waiting with the van by the fence to load it up.

It was hard work collecting the wood, but she persevered. Petunia did not care very much for any form of physical labour. She had waited, hoping that someone else would fetch it, but their supply had almost run out and it was made very obvious by others in the camp that she should take her turn to go to the yard.

She had filled a dozen bags, loaded them onto the trolley and dragged it to the hole in the fence where she left the bags and went back for another load. It was a warm, rather sultry evening and there were mosquitos everywhere, mainly around some rather stagnant puddles between huge tree trunks. She paused and listened and then hid behind the trunks as a train went by on the line adjacent to the yard. Next to the line was a small stream and she emerged to the very pleasant whiff of the meadowsweet that was growing by the stream.

Back at the woodpile, she once again sniffed and this time it was far from pleasant. The stench around her was revolting. She paused and thought maybe some small animal had crawled into the woodpile and died there. Spotting some perfect sized wood pieces at the back of the pile, she took two bags and climbed round to begin filling the bag. One bit of wood was stuck on something and she pulled it sharply. The stench of rotting flesh hit her like a blow. She stood back and saw a nail in the wood and a piece of black bin liner it had caught. She quickly took some smaller bits of wood from the edge of the pile and then began pulling some larger pieces for the campfire, but the stench became overpowering for a few seconds. There were flies everywhere, even coming out of the pile of wood. She took more bags from her pile nearby and hurriedly filled them. Suddenly, the wood pile began to collapse and some logs were rolling towards the ground. Then she saw what they had been covering, a large black bin bag. Big bluebottle flies were swarming out of a tear in it.

There were maggots wriggling to get out into the evening sunlight. It was then she saw the hand.

She stared at it for what seemed an eternity. It was certainly a human hand and it was sticking out of the black bin liner. She stood back and abruptly tripped over and fell onto the wood pile. She swore, struggled up and tried to think what she should do. She knew she should report it, but she couldn't and had no desire to be arrested and if she made a fuss, she knew that the travellers she was with would be very angry.

She went to the other side of the pile, filled several more bags and made two more journeys to the fence with the trolley. She only had a few more bags to fill. Avoiding that part of the pile, she took as much wood as she could and loaded the trolley again, and went back to the hole in the fence. The others had not yet arrived, but she knew they were on their way as she could hear the big ends of the engine knocking in one of the vans that were approaching.

She hastily ran back with the trolley to hide it and quickly looked around to make sure she had left no trace of herself. As she got back to the hole in the fence, the others were loading the bags into several vans. Reuben was stacking them inside their van and had left little room for her, so she had quite a squeeze getting into the front seat. The others ran off to get more vans and load them.

Reuben looked at her and said, "What's up? You look like shit, how did you cut your leg? It's bleeding."

"I tripped, that's all. I'll sort it when we get back. Look, I don't think we should go back there for a while. There's a body, a human one, in the wood pile. Let's get out of here, please?"

Reuben wondered what she had been taking that day. Petunia imagined a lot of strange things after using certain substances and she was inclined to make up fantastic stories to get attention.

"What are you on? There ain't no body, just a strange shaped bit of wood, I expect."

Petunia decided he was not in a particularly good mood with her and, as he obviously did not believe her, she wouldn't tell him any more.

Back at the camp some miles away, they unloaded the wood. The group seemed rather pleased, so she was thankful. She did not get on well with some of them and it was unusual for them to even be civil to her.

They had been very direct when telling her it was her turn to fetch firewood and she was glad it would not be her turn again for a while.

Petunia did not have very many clothes, nor was she that keen on washing them very often. She wiped the worst of the blood off her trousers with a piece of rag, and put a plaster on the cut and graze just below her knee. She then went to her supply of cannabis and made a reefer and put it in a secret place to smoke later. She cooked a meal for herself and Reuben and once they had eaten it, she smoked her reefer and went to bed.

Reuben, a surly silent man, got on with his chores, found his own cannabis and smoked some while he gazed into the glowing embers of their campfire. He thought of the next picture he would paint. He decided to start it the next morning, but he had no canvasses left. He would either have to go and buy some, which did not appeal to him, or source them another way. He knew of an art shop on the suburbs of the city not far away, but the canvasses he wanted were expensive. The woman who kept the shop always watched him like a hawk every time he went in there. He wondered if he could get some of the camp's children to distract her as he knew where she kept the things he wanted. He went over to another caravan and talked to that family about it. When he came back Petunia was fast asleep, so he went to a secret hiding place, got out the bottle of whiskey he had pinched from a corner store the day before and consumed most of it before falling asleep.

The next morning, he had forgotten what Petunia had said and so apparently had she. She was spaced out on something and was wandering around talking to herself. This was not unusual, so he left her to it and went into town with some of the other travellers.

Bob Moreby arrived at the timber yard at his normal time of eight-thirty. He unlocked the gates, drove in and having parked, he opened up the office. His mother came in a few minutes later and sat down at her desk. The phone rang, so he left her to it and went off to start the bench saw. He noticed the trolley was not where it was usually kept so he returned it to under the hydrangea. As he headed to the saw shed, he smelled the foul stench of rotting flesh. A swarm of flies flew up as he passed the firewood pile, which looked somewhat smaller than he remembered it the day before. He followed the stench round the back of the wood pile and saw the bin bag and then the hand sticking out of it.

Bob seldom hurried anywhere, but on this occasion, he almost ran back to the office, arriving breathless, sweating and most distressed. His mother was still on the phone and looked up at him in amazement as she listened to the caller. She wrote down the order she was taking, while Bob sat down in the chair opposite her.

It seemed an age before the phone was free. She put the receiver down and said, "What is the matter? You look like you have seen a ghost!"

"Phone 999. There's a body in the firewood pile. Looks and smells like it has been there a while."

Mrs Moreby knew her son did not play jokes and calmly rang 999 and told the police what he had said, and listened to their instructions, then gave her details and directions to the timber yard. She then hung up. She went to a cupboard, got out a bottle of brandy and poured one, which she handed to her son. He gulped it gratefully.

"It's horrible, mother. What did they say?"

"Not to let anyone in and wait until they get here. You go down to the gates, stop Bill and Darren coming in. Lock the gates up, wait until the cops get here. Don't let anyone in. I'll stop here. Did you see who it was?"

"No, I didn't. I don't want to neither. God knows how long it's been there. What I saw was bad enough. The hand was black and covered in maggots."

"Who could it be?"

"I dunno, not from round here anyway."

Bob helped himself to another brandy before going down to the gates.

The police arrived at the same time as the two other workers, Bill Birtwhistle and Darren. The police told them to go to the office. Bob took one of the police officers to the wood pile and pointed out what he had found.

He was retching and said, "I'll be in the office if you want me."

Another officer joined them and, holding a handkerchief to his mouth and nose, pulled away some of the bin bag. He backed off and called his control room on his radio. He said to the first policeman, "Right, you stop here, lad, don't let anyone near. Keep a log of times, people etcetera I'll go and ring control and tell them what we have is definitely a body and they can get the circus organized. No, lad, don't look to too close, it isn't nice. I'll get the details of the staff."

Before long, the 'circus' arrived. It consisted of a police surgeon, several scenes of crime officers and photographers, and some more uniform officers. The police surgeon having had a brief look and a smell said, "Dead, and for some time. I'll wait if I may in case there is more than one. Who's coming out?"

"Mr Catchpole I believe; he shouldn't be long."

"I'll speak to him before I go. Have we any idea who it might be?"

"None."

"Well, from the size of the hand and the clothes, I would say it is male, and been dead for at least a week, maybe more. I'll wait in the office."

Detective Chief Superintendent Saul Catchpole arrived about forty minutes later. Having donned a white set of overalls, he too looked at the body and said, "Have we taken photos?"

"Yes, sir, from every angle. Scenes of crime have cordoned off everything. Shall we uncover it?"

"Not yet, I would like the workers from here to tell me if there is anything odd, missing or altered in the area. Before we do, Alan can you get them? How many are there?

Alan Withers, the detective inspector, said, "Three men and one woman, who works in the office."

"Just ask them to come and look, will you, then we can get on with it."

Mrs Moreby looked round and said, "I wouldn't know. The only time I come down here is with messages. I don't have much to do with this lot."

Bob said, "Nor do I, really. We all just sort of do whatever, and when we have any offcuts or bits to use for firewood, we dump it on a pile here. There are often several piles. Then folk come and fill a bag and pay us at the office. I am sure it was a lot bigger yesterday. Looks like about twenty bags or more have been taken, but it may be the others sold a few bags before we closed last night."

Bill said, "Looks pretty normal to me. I did smell some'at the last few days, thought it were a rat, there are loads around. Bob's dog chases them sometimes, even catches a few."

Darren was looking at the pile and said, "I put a load on here yesterday and the day before. I load it with the big bucket on the tractor. I think there is quite a bit missing. I put the load on yesterday afternoon, quite late and unless someone came and bought some late in the afternoon, a lot has gone. I put some more there the day before. There were a few larger split lengths, four by fours. Most of them have gone. There was a lot of that reddish wood, that's gone too. The pile has certainly been moved about. I shovel up the loose bits round the edges, try to keep it as neat as I can. Now there are logs scattered everywhere. I wouldn't leave it like that."

Alan Withers said, "Did any of you move it at all?"

The three workers shook their heads. Darren said, "No, I don't know if anyone bought any yesterday afternoon, I wouldn't have seen. I was down with the grabber, moving tree trunks in the far end until I knocked off."

Saul said, "Thank you, all of you. All right, team, uncover it, please. Anything you find tell me straight away."

The young police officer, who had stalwartly kept a written record of visitors said, "Sir, over here, there is a little bit of blood, looks quite fresh, and some thread and a bit of fabric."

"Well done, thank you. We will bag it and look a bit further away while they are doing their job. Mr Moreby, are there any other piles like this in the yard?"

"Yes, several further down the yard."

"We will search them too, and in fact we need to search everywhere. My inspector will arrange for statements to be taken from you, and do you have keys for all the buildings? If you would be kind enough to show my inspector around? Right, lads, take the pile apart piece by piece."

The search of the yard took a long time. The scenes of crime officers put on masks and gloves as well as their sterile suits and began uncovering the body. The body was not firm, so they very carefully moved it inside the black bin liner and put it directly into a body bag. As the wood pile was taken apart, every piece was tagged and numbered and photographs were taken frequently. They called Saul Catchpole over when they uncovered three more black plastic bags at the bottom of the pile. Each were photographed and then carefully slit open to reveal each had a body inside. All were quite small and looked like children. Each was badly decomposed and the police surgeon was called back. After he had certified death the bodies were taken to the mortuary and the search continued.

Saul asked the doctor, "Any idea how they died?"

"Not at this stage, no,"

Saul called to Alan, "Have we any outstanding missing persons?"

"Not from round here. I've circulated what we have so far. I'm waiting to see if we get anything."

"What have you found out from the staff?"

"Quite a lot. The firewood pile is semi-constant there. People come, fill their bags with firewood and pay; usually it works out about a pound per bag. No names and addresses are taken, but the lady knows most of the regulars, if not by name, by their cars, or by sight. Most of them are fairly local. She has done a list of those she does know. In fact, one chap turned up wanting some and Julia is talking to him now. He comes about once a fortnight. She asked him if he saw or smelled anything when he last came. He said the pile was very small last time and he almost cleared it, there were only a few logs left. He has given us the names of several other customers he knows."

"What about other staff and regular visitors?"

"She has given us all she can think of. I've spoken to both Bill and the other chap and they say it is the smaller branches and bits of offcuts put on there. Mainly from the last fortnight. They had a big order from a building supplier and the offcuts were put on the pile. That would be the four by four lengths."

"Who else would have access to the yard?"

"During opening hours, no one who isn't spotted by the staff. The premises aren't secure though, we found a gap in the fence not far from the gate and it has been used very recently. There are a few stray bits of wood there. The fence looks as if it has been recently cut. We also found some more recent blood and some material like that we found near the pile. We have taken some footprints too. There is another way in, it is locked, but it doesn't look as if it has been used in a long time, from the railway line."

"Can we check if any train drivers saw anything?"

"Already underway. I have asked the transport police to help. I have sent officers to the nearby auction mart, the agricultural suppliers and the farm supplies in the road leading to here. We've started house to house in the village and there is someone checking at the two garages and getting their security camera footage. "

"Thanks, Alan, now we had better find out who our victims are. Can I leave you here, to supervise and I'll ring the coroner and get down to the morgue?"

" Sure, I'll meet you back at the office. What about the press?"

"I'll do that tomorrow, when we know a bit more."

Having checked that the premises would be suitably guarded, Saul drove back to his office, made several phone calls and then went down to the mortuary. The mortuary attendant was a man Saul had known for many years. George was a large cheerful man who was very efficient. He looked up as Saul walked in through the door and said, "Thought we'd be seeing you soon, Mr Catchpole, keeping well, are you?"

"Not too bad, thanks, George. How are you and your Missus and that lad of yours, Stewart, isn't it? Did you not tell me he was going to join the army?"

"Well, fancy you are remembering that, yes, he got into the Paras and I'm right proud of him. He loves it. We have a new pathologist just moved up from the smoke I think, oh here he is. Mr Newton may I introduce Mr Catchpole, the senior policeman round here."

"Pleased to meet you, are you intending to stay? It will take a while and your lads are here, just suiting up."

"I think I had better, I might learn something interesting."

"Yes, well, if you must, but if you are going to faint or be sick, do it outside."

"Mr Catchpole won't be sick or owt like that. He has a cast iron stomach, well known for it, is that not so, sir?"

"Not quite, never at a post-mortem, but I was very sick after a blow on the head fairly recently."

"Well, so long as you don't get in my way. Your scenes of crime officers are just coming in. They can bag everything and put exhibit numbers on. Now the first one, this looks like a woman, very small indeed, yes there are wisdom teeth so an adult, so she is over twenty-six, I estimate, more possibly."

For the next two hours Mr Newton and his assistant told and showed Saul and the scenes of crime officers many interesting things. George was assisting them, happily singing to himself as he cleared away maggots, flies and other detritus, and bagging some up as requested by either Saul or the pathologists. Numerous samples were taken for later analysis.

When Saul left, he went home, had a shower. Changed and smelling much better he went into the office, where a lot of his team were collecting, having spent the day on numerous enquiries.

Alan Withers had collated their results and was allocating follow up tasks for the following day. Saul checked if there was anything urgent needing his attention and then went home.

The next morning, as Saul came in, Alan smiled and said, "OK, everyone, meeting and talk through in fifteen minutes," and he then followed Saul into his office.

"Any problems, Alan?"

"Dozens, but nothing we cannot cover. What have you found out?"

"A lot. Nothing to tell us their names yet. I'll brief everyone, is the coffee pot on?"

"Yes."

At the briefing Saul confirmed there were four victims, two adults and two children, and the pathologist thought they were related; certainly the male was related to the children as they shared a rather rare abnormality in the little fingers; and that they were all shot, in the head, at least twice. Even the toddler. The bullets had gone off to the lab and were thought to be 9mm. He then asked, "Have we any missing persons that answer this?"

Paul, one of the detective sergeants said, "Not as yet. There are, as you know, always lots, but not a group of four, or a family. How long have they been dead?"

Saul replied, "Less than two weeks, and they were killed elsewhere. Lividity suggests the man lay on his front for some time before being moved. Anything new from the wood yard?"

"Yes, we think we found where they might have been killed. The forensic lads are going over it now. At the far end of the yard is another of those single-story brick buildings, like the office. It has a cellar, which the office does not have. The manager says it hasn't been used in years, as it is damp, and there is a massive crack all down the back wall and the floor is rotten in places. The manager says it hasn't been used, but it has. There is rather a lot of what looks like blood and the remains of what looks like human faeces in a corner. There is no lock on the door but the SOCO chap thinks it has been sealed with a chain and padlock. He has found marks that can identify the chain if we can find it."

"You are suggesting that someone has been held prisoner there?"

"It looks like it, which means we have to look very closely at the staff."

"And?"

"And it is rather interesting. The mother has no form, at all. The manager, Robert Moreby, had an old conviction for drink driving, but also flagged up for suspected fraud and tax avoidance offences. No convictions but he was investigated about seven years back. The younger lad, Darren, he openly told us he has a conviction for criminal damage three years ago and he explained he was a stupid irresponsible youth then. He then said he met the right woman, has grown up, calmed down got married. They have a baby now and he has gone utterly straight since then."

"And the older chap, Bill Birtwhistle?"

"There is something I don't like about him. He has form, lots of it, all some time ago, robbery, theft, taking without consent, and he has been inside a couple of times. He came out of prison ten years ago, and since that time, nothing,"

"What did he say about it?"

"Well he didn't volunteer it and when I asked him why, he said that the Moresbys didn't know about it. He then went on to say it was a long time ago, in another area and he'd left it all behind. He is not a married man, he lives alone, in a small room above a café in the village. I asked to search it, and he shrugged his shoulders, and said if he said no, I'd get a warrant and do it anyway and to go ahead. There is nothing there, and I mean nothing, No books, no post, no personal things, just the basics, electric kettle, two mugs, two plates and a few ashtrays. He said he never gets any post and has no friends. He does spend quite a lot of time drinking at the Black Horse of an evening. "

"Has he a vehicle?"

"Yes, and I searched that too. Full of fag ends, empty fag packets, but otherwise empty. I did find a single key and asked him about it. He said he'd found it in the yard, meant to hand it in at the office but forgot. It was under the front passenger seat under the carpet."

"Interesting, tell me what you think."

"I think he has somewhere else that he goes to. To be honest he gives me the creeps.

"Then we had better find what that key fits for a start. Do they have lockers at the yard?"

"Not as such, no, but there is a small room that they use as a kitchen dining room. Untidy but nothing untoward in there."

"Has anyone traced any visitors, anyone taking wood from the pile?

Alan said, "A few, but I think most of the customers will come forward, if we appeal in the press. No one came for any wood yesterday, and it looks like the wood was taken in the evening, stolen, and I suspect that whoever took it must have uncovered the body."

"Was anyone seen in the area the day before yesterday?"

"Only some new age travellers in the village. Several were in the Black Horse until about eight p.m., when they left."

"Do we know where they are camped up?"

"Not yet, I've asked the local stations to find out."

"Have you drafted a press release?"

"Not yet."

"Then we will do it after the meeting."

Chapter 2

Saul made an appeal on the local television and with the local press for anyone with any information to come forward if they had seen anyone near the woodyard. It went out and the office staff were inundated with calls from all over the country. The office managers, Fred Dunlop and Nita, weeded out the most promising ones, and started following them up. In the mid-afternoon they had a break and exchanged information. Nita said, "Sir, we have a family missing from down south, Hertfordshire, mother, father, seven-year-old boy and a girl, just one. They were on holiday up here, but the mother's sister hasn't heard from them for over a week. A local officer is seeing her now. They were due back from the holiday tomorrow. A hotel manager near there says the same family never turned up, even though they had sent a deposit when they booked. That was eleven days ago."

"Do we know what vehicle they were using?" Saul asked.

"Not yet, they didn't own a car. They hired one, not sure where from."

"Any more interesting leads?"

"About two dozen that buy their firewood from there have called, and we are working through them."

"Thanks. Alan. Look, I have a dental appointment in an hour, will you cover for me until I get back?"

"Sure I will. Have you time for a quick chat before you go?"

"Yes, of course, shut the door!"

Alan sat down and said, "Saul, you know Caroline and I are getting married?"

"Yes, and I am delighted for you both."

"Will it mean she or I must move away from the squad?"

"Not unless either of you want to. Actually, I am a bit ahead of you. I have already notified personnel that I need you both on the squad, and I do not see it will affect your work in any way."

"Thank you, er, Saul, will you do me the honour of being my best man?"

"I would love to. When?"

"Next month. I'll be straight with you; we want to start a family. Once we have a child Caroline does not want to return to work, at least until the children are well old enough. I earn enough to keep us. You are bringing all your family to the wedding?"

"I hope so, really all of them?"

"Yes, especially Diana and your brother."

"I am sure they would be delighted. Where are you going to live?"

"That's the other thing I needed to talk to you about. You know my foster parents were quite well off, well they left me quite a lot of money and it is more than enough for a decent place."

"Good, it helps to have a nice house."

"I have not needed a big place before, but now I do. We have looked at a lot and the one we fancy is three doors down from yours. Would you have a problem with that?"

"No, not at all but thank you for asking. I'd be delighted. I know Anna will be thrilled and would, in due course, love to babysit from time to time."

"Thank you it is just, well, how do I put it. I am only a DI. The house is expensive. Are others going to think I am sucking up to you?"

"I see what you mean. No, I'll make sure they don't. You have never made a secret of your background. The street is a good investment, we moved there about ten years ago. You mean Mr Petrovitch's house?"

"Yes, it will need a bit of a face lift."

"Which I will enjoy helping you with. I think my brother might too."

"Thanks. I don't expect that, but I could use your advice. The garden will need a lot of work. At the moment, it has huge greenhouses, rather neglected. We will have to get rid of most of them."

"Yes, he grew hundreds of fuchsias in them. I know who will buy the greenhouses."

"Who"

"My sister-in-law, Diana. She will want them for her orchids. I wouldn't mind buying one either, for my orchid collection."

"Maybe we can discuss that later. You know that I don't really have any family?"

"Apart from your mother, yes, you said,"

"Caroline has a big family, so one side of the church will be almost empty, could I borrow yours?"

"I doubt you would want my younger brother, or my parents, but my kids, and their partners, would be delighted to fill your side of the church, and most of the squad will be there, with their partners if you invite them."

"They will want to come?"

"Of course they will. They work with both of you."

"Thanks, Saul, I really owe you and your family."

"No, you don't. Anna was saying only last night that she considers you an extra son, I do too. Sam said that it is like having another brother. Stephen asked me if you would consider being the new baby's godfather. I said I would ask you; the child is due any day now."

"I would love to, that is a compliment. So do we know what it is yet?"

"Yes, Lissa asked. It is another boy, a brother for Benjamin."

"Have they decided on a name?"

"Yes, but I don't approve, but I dare not say so."

"Go on…"

"They want to call the poor boy Saul, Saul Peter. I told them that having been given that name I had a hard time at school, and afterwards."

"I rather like it, I hate Alan, I wanted an unusual name, but Dad said I would always be Alan to him. I wanted Luke."

"Good name. Look, I must get down to the dentist. It is hell finding a parking spot."

"I'll drop you off. Ring me when you need picking up."

"It's all right, I'll catch a bus."

"No. Please don't. Look what happened last time. You and buses don't mix. Are you likely to be long?"

"Probably, I think at least one tooth needs to come out."

"Then ring me."

Saul had to have two molars out and was feeling pretty groggy as he came out of the dentist's surgery. His mouth was numb, and he had bled rather a lot. The dentist, a splendid chap called Miles, who was an ex-Royal Navy man, and a very good dentist, had told him to go home and rest quietly. Then Miles added, "I know you; you will go back to the vital work you do, and just carry on. Here, a few pain killers if you need them, you probably will."

Saul walked along the pavement and approached the busy town centre and thought about ringing Alan, but then decided to walk quietly at least some of the way. He needed to clear his head, so he walked up through the shopping precinct. Feeling a bit lightheaded, he sat down outside a café and ordered a coffee. His jaw was just starting to hurt, so he took one of the pain killers he had been given, with the drink. After about ten minutes he began to feel a little better, so he ordered another coffee, and waited for the pain killer to kick in, and contemplated that Miles knew him just a little too well.

As he sat and began to relax in the sunshine, he heard a commotion a little way down the street. He stood up and saw a young policeman struggling with a large man who then hit the policeman hard and broke away from his grip. The man ran towards Saul, as the policeman struggled to his feet and shouted, "Stop him." Saul saw that the officer was bleeding from the mouth and nose.

Several women got hastily out of the way of the violent man, leaving three men and a teenage youth in the running man's path. Two of the men rapidly disappeared, and the remaining one was a smartly dressed chap of about five foot four. Saul joined him and the youth, and as the man rushed towards them, the youth did a splendid rugby tackle that brought the man down, the businessman grabbed an arm as they managed to hold him. Saul quickly handcuffed both the arms behind the struggling man's back. The man continued to resist violently, but with three people restraining him he failed to break free.

The policeman, who to Saul looked about fifteen, joined them and said to the man, "You are under arrest for theft and assault on police. Calm down."

The policeman then cautioned him and looked up at Saul, who said, "It's all right, Officer, I have cuffed him. I'll hold on to him, are you all right?"

"Bit shaky, sir, but I'll live. Who are you?"

"Detective Chief Superintendent Catchpole. Is help on its way?"

"Yes, sir."

The four of them restrained the man until a police van arrived and he was put in the back. Saul then turned to the young officer and said, "You need to go to hospital, lad. Sergeant, this young officer has a nasty blow to the head, I saw it. I'll take the details of these two brave gentlemen and I will come down to Main Street Bridewell. I need my cuffs anyway."

The sergeant, who obviously recognized Saul, said, "Thank you, sir."

Saul turned to the youth and the businessman and said, "Thank you so much for your timely assistance, very brave both of you. I trust you are not hurt, no? Well, may I take your details so we can thank you properly?"

"Not at all, I had to do something."

The youth said, "So did I, I saw him thump the copper and that's not right."

Saul walked with them back to his table and said, "Can I offer you a drink? I was having one anyway. I need to pay the bill. Would you join me?" Saul ordered drinks and took their details. "I will ensure that you are thanked. Colin, how old are you?"

"Sixteen. I want to be a police officer when I leave college."

"Not a professional rugby player? That was an impressive tackle."

"Yes, I play a bit, but I want to be a police officer, always have done."

"And you, sir, may I ask what it is you do?"

"I'm a salesman. I sell jewellery. I was mugged in London last year. One woman came to my assistance and because of what she did they caught them. I felt it was the least I could do. I think you must be a very senior detective?"

"Yes, my name is Saul Catchpole. I am the officer in charge of a murder squad."

They finished their drinks and after they had gone Saul paid the bill and, feeling a bit better, as the pain killer had started to kick in, he walked down to the Main Street police station, and made his way to the cells. The custody sergeant, who he knew, handed him his cuffs and said, "Thanks for your help, sir. The young PC has a broken nose and two loose teeth."

"Poor kid, he did very well. I was impressed. Was there another officer with him?"

"I have yet to find out. He is a brand new probationer and it was his first shoplifter; in fact, it may have been his first arrest. His tutor is getting another statement. That is one of the questions I want to ask her."

"I think I might too. I'll make my statement and send it over to you. What was it all about?"

"He's a traveller and artist, so he says. He and a load of kids went into an art shop and while the kids tried to distract the lady, he took six quite expensive canvasses and ran out with them. The two officers were just round the corner, spotted him and stopped him. They called for backup, and he seemed compliant. The WPC went back to the shop to get details and he took off. We got the canvasses."

"She is his tutor? She should have known better."

"Only for today. His regular tutor had to go to a funeral. She was the only non-probationer free on the shift."

"I see. Here are the two witnesses' details. They were very helpful. He's a big man, I doubt I could have held him on my own. A traveller, you say, what is his name?"

"He refuses to say. He has a tattoo of Reuben on his hand and on his forearm, one of Petunia."

"When you find out where he is living, let me know, will you? I am looking for a group of them."

"Certainly, I saw the circulation. Do you want scenes of crime to check his clothes?"

"Yes, please, and get a DNA sample. I did notice he stank of something, smelled like petunia oil."

"I wouldn't know what that smelled like, but I think he is also as high as a kite on something. Sir, are you all right, you look a little unwell, you seem very pale?"

"No, I'm OK. I had just had two teeth out. I was having a drink at a café before going back to the office. I'll head back there now."

"I'll get you a lift, sir."

"No, please don't! If you do, I will never hear the last of it. Last time my DI let me out on my own I came across a robbery on a bus. There were bus jokes for ages. Now it will be shoplifter jokes. Just at the moment, I can do without it."

"Understood, sir. They'll find out, they always do."

"Hopefully when I am feeling a bit better. Thanks, skipper, I will email a copy of my statement through."

Saul walked back to the office and on arriving, met Alan who looked at him and said, "You need to go home, you should have rung me, come on I'll drive you home."

"I have to do a statement first. Then I'll go. This is urgent. While I do that, update me?"

"OK, it looks like it is this family from Hertfordshire. We have found the hire car they used, parked in the nearby auction mart car park, hidden behind some bushes. We have brought it in, and they are going over it now. We have the dental records being sent up. It looks like they are the Stevens family, from Hitchin. I think we will need a dental identification. We have some clothes, too. Is this statement that urgent? You do not look too good. What have you been doing?"

"Yes, it is, and I will tell you later. Do you need me for anything else?"

"No, I can handle it, er, you haven't been on a bus again, have you?"

"No. Leave it, Alan, I'm not in the mood."

"Will you be fit to drive?"

"Yes, now leave me alone!"

Saul wrote his statement, completed his notebook and emailed a copy to the custody officer. He was about to put the original statement in the internal post when there was a knock on the door. He opened it and a uniform WPC was there.

"I am WPC Wright, sir. Main Street. I understand you wished to speak to me?"

"Yes, I do. Come in. Shut the door. Here is my statement. Now tell me, what happened?"

"I made a serious mistake. The man seemed compliant, and happy to wait for transport. I left him with the probationer while I went back to get a phone number. I shouldn't have done; I see that now."

"The result of which was a serious assault on Neville Brown, a brand-new probationer, an escaped prisoner, and a lot of trouble. Why was he not cuffed? I take it he was searched?"

"Yes, Nev did that. He said he would come quietly. I was so wrong, and I am so sorry."

"Yes, you were, hardly the way to guide a new officer, is it?"

"No sir, I feel awful about it."

"Good. How much service have you got?"

"Four years, sir."

"Enough to know better then. Thankfully he did very well and the three of us got your prisoner back. You owe that young man."

"I know it, sir. We have got a name for the prisoner now, Sergeant Stubbs said you wanted to know. He calls himself Reuben and admitted his partner is called Petunia. We are doing fingerprints and DNA now."

"Will you send me a copy of the results?"

"Of course, sir. I really am sorry. It has taught me a lesson too. Are you going to stick me on a disciplinary?"

"Not this time, no. Learn from it. We all make mistakes. Thank you for coming to see me. I am sure you will make sure young Brown gets everything he needs until he is fit for duty again?"

"Yes, sir, it is the least I can do. One other thing, I went back to the art shop. The proprietor there says she thinks he is an artist called Reuben. He has sold a lot of pictures at Appleby Horse Fair. His partner is a sculptress, Petunia. May I ask question?"

"Of course. Look, sit down, child, you look terrified, I am not an ogre, despite what you may have been told."

"You are investigating the four bodies found in the timber yard?"

"I am."

"We had the posters delivered for putting out on noticeboards. They were in a pile in the custody suite corridor. Reuben saw one and then went pale. I saw him then look at one in the charge room. He read it through. I asked him if he knew anything about it and he said no. He won't give us an address or where he is staying or a full name or anything."

"So, he will stay in custody until he does then."

"I wondered if he was waiting, so the people he is travelling with can get away. He seemed resigned to staying in, but only after he had seen that poster."

"Interesting. Now, I am about to head home. Do you need a lift back to your nick?"

"That is kind of you, sir, yes please. Thank you for being so nice about it. I was going to go and see Neville at the general hospital. I went off duty about half an hour ago."

"I'll drop you off there then, I have to pass it on my way home."

As they got to Saul's car, he realized he was feeling a lot better, and the pain killers had obviously worked. He rather liked WPC Wright. Once in the car they headed out into the traffic and promptly got stuck in a traffic jam. He asked her what had caused her to get it wrong. She admitted she was splitting up wither policeman partner, who wanted her to stay at home and not continue with her police career. She told Saul she wanted to be on CID, and that her partner was a traffic officer and had used his friend and colleagues to stop her getting any further.

Saul asked her what she intended to do. She told him she was trying to leave, but all her money had gone out of her joint account with her partner and that she was in a bad situation because of it.

"So, what are you intending to do? Have you any children?"

"No, I have no family, not close, so I am stuck. I was going to see a solicitor, but the one we used is definitely on Tony's side."

"Have you told your inspector?"

"No, he is Tony's friend as well."

"Then will you let me help you? Are you not the WPC Wright that dealt with that criminal libel case, while you were on an aide last year?"

"Yes, sir I really enjoyed that aide, but Tony hated me not being at home to cook and clean for him. I know, he is a control freak. I can't think why I didn't see it before. I think I finally fell out of love with him a couple of months ago.

"It's Sharon, isn't it? Tell me honestly, has he been violent towards you?"

Sharon turned her head and looked out of the window for a long time and when she turned back her saw tears in her eyes.

"Has he?"

"Yes, sir. He is very clever about it, doesn't hit me where it will show. I have had enough and now he's making work difficult for me too."

"Then you need to get out. You know senior officers are not just there to jump on you when things go wrong. We can help. If I find somewhere for you to stay for a while, how long will it take you to pack?"

"It is already done, but I can't afford much, all the money I had saved has gone from the account."

"Do you want to take him to court?"

"Not really, I just want out."

"Then write down your details, phone number, address, and his details as well. I will talk to someone. I will get back to you by this evening. I am sure I can help."

"That is damn decent of you, but won't I get into trouble by telling you? Won't it make things worse?"

"No, Sharon, it won't. It looks like we are finally moving, I will drop you off at the hospital and then go home. In the door pocket by you are my details, on that card."

"Thanks, but why are you being so kind?"

"Someone has to be concerned for your welfare, and it is obvious that your supervisors are not."

He dropped her off by the hospital and then drove back to his office. Alan looked very surprised to see him coming in but waited until he was free to speak to him.

Saul shut his office door and rang his sister in law, "Diana, it's Saul. Do you still have that little farm workers' cottage empty?"

"Yes, Saul, why, do you want it for something?"

"Can I bring you a lame duck?"

"Yes. Male or female, and needing friendship and protection?"

"Female, needing both. Partner problems. I am sorry to ask, she needs to move today and has little or no money."

"She won't need any. We just want it lived in. I'll get it ready. One of us?"

"Yes. Her name is Sharon Wright. I'll explain when we get there."

"I'll get some supplies in, the water on and the phone put back on."

"Thanks Diana."

Chapter 3

Saul made a few phone calls, then made himself a coffee and rather tersely explained to Alan that he couldn't be disturbed. A few minutes later some files were delivered to his office. They were the files for both Sharon and Tony Gilchrist. Soon another superintendent, a friend of his, arrived. Saul waved him into a chair and said, "Wally, thanks for coming, I need your advice. I've hit a problem, and as head of discipline, you need to know this. "

Wally looked at the file on Saul's desk and said, "Not Gilchrist again. That man seems to live a charmed life. I think he has friends in very high places. He has an appalling record, especially with women. Twice I have recommended that he be required to resign, twice I have been ignored. What's this about, Saul?"

Saul told him. Together they looked at both the files, Saul said, "Of course, I've only heard her side and there are always two sides. Until about six months ago she was outstanding then she moved to the station and apparently the shift she is on now. Do you know the reason for that?"

"Actually, I think I do. If I'm not mistaken, three female officers resigned from that station within a month. I don't know what shift they were on, but they were not the only ones. Quite a few women have left after serving there over the last three or four years. I'll find out. Obviously, I need to move her immediately; not sure where I can put her."

"I need an aide on my squad and I can keep an eye on things too. I've already arranged alternative accommodation for her as from this evening. She'll be safe there, I can assure you. Her new address should not be made available to anyone.

"All right, but I do need a contact number."

"Use mine. Tell her to report to my office in the morning. We'll get her things together from her station after that. I'll want you there!"

"Fair enough, of course I will be."

Saul rang Sharon's number from the office phone and put it on record and loudspeaker. It was answered very quickly.

"Are you alone, Sharon? It's Saul Catchpole."

"No, not at the moment"

"Can you talk"

"No."

"Is he there?"

"Yes."

"Are you in danger?"

"Yes."

"At your place?"

"Yes."

"I'll be there asap. Are you packed?"

"Yes, thanks."

Leaving Wally to listen in and arrange help, Saul gathered his things, ran down to his car and drove as fast as he could to Sharon's house. He noticed a traffic police car parked outside. As he approached the house, he could hear a man shouting inside. On the path were a number of suitcases and bags.

He went up to the front door, listened and turned his mobile phone on to record.

"You aren't going anywhere, you little bitch. You'll come crawling back when you can't find anywhere to stay. Nor will you get into CID, I've made sure of that. It might teach you to defy me!"

Saul was relieved to hear Sharon say, "Look, Tony, I've told you; I am going. You've beaten me up once too often. You may think you have control, but you don't. Accept it; I'm walking away from you, this house and our relationship. I like my job and intend to continue with it. You think your friends can stop me; you're wrong. Tony, you're drunk. Back off and let me leave."

"Wherever you go, I will find you. You can't accept it, can you, that women have no place in the police? You will never get anywhere; I've made sure of that. Stay here, get a proper woman's job and keep house for me."

"In your dreams, Tony. You keep telling me about all your friends, but have you considered I might have supporters too? It's over. Go and live with one of your mistresses. You thought I didn't know? Of course, I did.

Has it occurred to you that I know rather too much about you? Is that why you're scared of me leaving? Think I might tell someone?"

"Who was it that rang just now, a boyfriend?"

"No. Just someone from work."

"I know where you go, I'm told. I have friends."

" Yes, so have I. Now let me pass. Please don't hit me again, Tony, no!"

Saul had listened to this confrontation with growing anger. He pushed gently on the front door and was a bit surprised when it opened. He moved silently into the hallway and standing with his back to him was a large police officer in uniform who was moving towards Sharon with his clenched fist raised and starting to throw a punch. Saul grabbed the wrist and as he did so he saw the man's other hand grab Sharon by the hair. The man, very startled, let go of her and turned aggressively trying to break free of Saul's grip. Saul said, "That's enough. You are under arrest for assault. Don't even think of hitting me."

Gilchrist tried to throw a punch at Saul, who neatly ducked.

"Who are you? Get out of my house. You can't arrest me, I am the police."

"So am I, and a lot more senior than you are."

"Well you're trespassing."

"Actually, I was invited. You stink of booze, calm down and give me your other wrist. Either that or I'll use my CS gas spray."

Saul used his free hand to take the spray, that he always carried while on duty, from his belt and pointed it at Gilchrist. Saul also noticed that a police utility belt was on the ground by their feet with the asp truncheon racked up and with a bit of blood on it. He glanced at Sharon and saw she was bleeding from the mouth and nose.

"All right, granddad, impress me, who are you? Some jumped up detective from another force? I've never met you and I know most of the detectives round here."

Sharon kicked the asp out of reach and saw Saul raise the spray to the right level and then made a dash to the kitchen to get out of the way.

Saul had never used the spray in anger, only at training courses, but hoped fervently that he could use it on this occasion.

"Stand back, or I will use it. This is your final warning."

"Silly old goat, it's not a real one, and you're not a copper!"

Gilchrist rushed towards Saul and, as he did so, Saul gave him the recommended three second spray. Saul stepped back as the man was still coming for him, and then the spray took effect. Gilchrist spluttered, sneezed and then put his hands to his eyes. Saul quickly stepped back out of the front door as he could feel the effects of the spray himself. He managed to grab Gilchrist and pull him out with him. Sharon joined him and handed him the pair of handcuffs that had been on the utility belt on the floor. Together they cuffed him and put him on the ground. Sharon took the radio from him, called for help and as they almost sat on Gilchrist, Saul cautioned him. He then said, "Are you all right, Sharon? I got here as quick as I could."

"Just about, how are you?"

"Eyes watering a bit, but fine. I must admit I never realized that could feel so good."

"He went crackers, I wasn't expecting him back, I think he was trying to lock me in."

"I heard a bit of it, even got it recorded. Looks like help is arriving. Do you need an ambulance?"

"No, I'll heal."

"Good; but this time he does go to court, I saw and heard enough. Lie still, you stupid man, or you'll hurt yourself!"

Tony, spluttering and coughing, managed to get out a string of expletives and then said, "Who the hell are you?"

"My name is Catchpole. You're in deep trouble. Here, officer, help us!"

"Yes, sir, of course. Sir, what happened?"

"I have arrested him for ABH, and he resisted, so I sprayed him. Put him in the van."

An inspector, who had arrived with three more policemen looked at Sharon and said, "Sharon, isn't it? Here, let's help you back inside."

"No, I'd rather stay out here. It's full of CS gas in there! Let's go around the back to the kitchen and I'll open some windows."

Saul wiped his face and eyes, watched as Gilchrist was placed in the back of the police van. He turned to a sergeant and said, "He drove here in that traffic car. He stinks of booze. Get him breathalysed. The car keys are on the hall table, you'll need to get someone to take it away."

The sergeant said, "Yes, sir, I can do that. I am authorized. Are you and the lady all right?"

"I am, I'm not so sure about her. Get him away from here and then I'll catch up with you."

Back in the kitchen of the house, Sharon was sitting at the table with the inspector. Saul came in and sat down and said, "Are you from her station?"

"No, sir, I'm from Roundhay station. I have been here before, however. Last month, a neighbour called us. He was smashing the place up. She wasn't here and he wouldn't let us in. He was drunk then. I spoke to his inspector about him."

A woman knocked on the open backdoor and tentatively came in.

"I'm from next door. I called you. I was worried. Can I help at all?

"Thank you, Gladys, so much. I feel so embarrassed and ashamed. He really went mad this time."

"Not for the first time either, ducks. Here, lovey, calm down. You've no need to be ashamed. You've done nothing wrong. I don' know who you gentlemen are, but it's about time someone stopped the nasty bully. She came in to see me not long ago and he pushed his way in and dragged her back. He threatened me and my Sid then, so we rang the nick. She's been a good neighbour to us, he has not. I've been frightened for you, pet!"

The inspector said, "Will you give evidence?"

"Yes, we both will if Sharon wants us to. So will Lydia who lives on the other side. She can't stay here though, he'll be back."

Saul said, "She won't be here; I've found somewhere else for her to stay."

"He'll find her, he says he always can. You take care of her, none of you have, so far."

"I know, but this time she will be safe, you have my word on it."

"Well, who are you?"

Inspector Harmer said, "Mr Catchpole is a very senior officer."

"Well, you lot haven't done very well so far, have you?"

"No, we haven't. I am ashamed that someone like PC Gilchrist is still a police officer. He won't be much longer, I can assure you. Sharon, do you have a car?"

"Yes, the old blue Peugeot outside."

"Right, have your tea, collect everything, and I mean everything you want or need, and then I'll arrange to come with you to a safe house. Gladys, could you help her?"

"Of course I will. Come on, dearie, let's get your things. Does you want to take your cat? If not, he can stop with me for a few days."

"I doubt if I can. He's upstairs in the spare room in his basket."

"Yes, you can, I'm certain he'll be welcome where you're going. Oh, Wally, through here please."

Wally came in with two plain clothes officers and said, "Saul, let me deal with this. Has she seen a doctor? The postings are sorted like you asked."

"Not yet. I'm taking her to that safe place I spoke about. Will you clean up here while I get her away? In his case, he won't be going anywhere, he'll be suspended. Sharon, go with Superintendent Evans here, tell him everything, make a statement, see a doctor. I'll be back to move you in about an hour. Inspector, someone needs to stay here. If, as I suspect, he has friends who are low enough to help him, I don't want this place being smashed up."

"Right, sir."

Saul finished his tea, taking another pain killer as he did so, thanked Gladys and gave her his card. She looked at it and said, "You is senior! You do something about this!"

"Yes, madam, I certainly will. I only found out what was going on this afternoon."

"I'll let *you* off then, but protect her!"

He drove his car to the local station, wrote a statement, transferred his recording from his phone, and said to the duty inspector, "You know who I am."

"Yes, of course, sir."

"You are not connected to either WPC Wright or PC Gilchrist?"

"No, sir."

"Then come with me, I wish to see Gilchrist."

They got to the cells where Gilchrist was being held and went into the cell to talk to him. The custody officer, who Saul had known for years, accompanied them.

The inspector said, "You've met Mr Catchpole, I take it?"

"Yes, unfortunately. He reckons he's some senior officer, but I doubt it."

The custody officer smiled and said, "Oh, I can assure you he is, very senior."

Gilchrist said, "Prove it."

Saul took out his warrant card and handed it to the custody sergeant who showed it to Gilchrist, who, looking rather shocked, glared at Saul.

"PC Gilchrist, I have several things to say to you. You are not fit to wear that uniform. You have been drinking, on duty and driving a police car. Your violence and threatening behaviour is totally unacceptable. WPC Wright has left your house and will not be returning there. Any attempt by you or your so-called friends to harass or intimidate her or anyone helping her, or any witnesses, will be treated with the utmost severity. Don't try to find her, she has already been posted elsewhere. Superintendent Evans, from discipline and complaints, will be dealing with the many discipline matters."

"But she's my partner, she'll come back; she's mine!"

"That will be her choice, made freely. I hope you have another profession to fall back on, because your police service is at an end."

"You can't do that!"

"Watch me. I will certainly try. Inspector, ensure he is given all his legal rights and find something else for him to wear. He's not fit to wear that uniform."

Having arranged things with Wally, Saul was picked up and returned to Sharon's house. He got out of the large van he had arrived in and went in through the open front door, together with the two uniformed PCs that had come with him. He found Sharon in the kitchen. He explained to Sharon that he trusted both the officers and had known them for years and that they had no contact with anyone from her station or traffic.

"Sharon, do you want to go? If you don't, tell me now?"

"Yes, please, I do, I really do. I'm never coming back here. Where am I going, a women's refuge?"

"No, I've found a nice little cottage for you, where you'll be safe. Can I come in your car with you and your stuff will go in the back of the van outside with these two officers. It's all right, they don't know Tony. I'll explain on the way. Do you have everything? Keys, jewellery, car documents?"

"Yes, all that, I even have my CD player, my telly, insurance, and everything. Are you sure about the cat? Gladys said she'd have it if I couldn't, but we worry that if Tony sees it, he'll hurt it just to get at me?"

"No, it's all right, I know you can have it where we're going. I'm not saying where until we're en route."

Having loaded everything up, they locked the house and departed about half an hour later. The van followed them as they left the city. When they came to a large layby on the long straight road, Saul said, "Pull over and wait. I want to check no one is following us. Now, the reason I wouldn't say where we're going is it occurred to me that the house may have been bugged."

"I never thought of that, but actually it might explain a few things, like him knowing who I'd been talking to on the phone or when I had gone out and not told him where I was going. The bastard!"

"We'll soon see. Now, Sharon, I need you to tell me, am I pushing you into something you don't really want? Will you let me help you? I can get you the help you need."

"No, you're rescuing me. You can't think much of me, letting him do this to me. I'm to blame as well. I should have been stronger. I deal with this every day at work, but I didn't take my own advice. I did love him, but not anymore. I'm just frightened of him and his mates and what they will do. He does have some pretty influential mates."

"Not influential enough. I need the truth. Sharon, do you have anyone else?"

"No, no one, his jealousy made sure of that. I've gone off relationships for a while. What I don't understand is why you are being so kind. Almost like a father, if I still had one. My parents both died a few years back. In a car crash, which Tony dealt with, that was how I met him. I suppose he knew I didn't have anyone else to go to."

"I see. Why? I am doing my job. You've been let down badly, by your supervisors. I looked at your service record. You have ability, dedication and intelligence. I'll tell you what I have arranged, but if you're not happy with it, you must say so. As from now, you are on an indefinite AIDE to the CID on the murder squad. I will be your ultimate supervisor, and you'll be working on my team. Do well, and it may open some doors for you. If it isn't to your liking, then we'll have a rethink. Personally, I'm taking you to a charming cottage on a farm owned by my brother and his wife. They are Jake and Diana Catchpole. Both of them are more than capable of protecting you, Diana especially. She was an officer herself and is also more than what she seems. She knows you are coming and welcomes you. How are you with rural life?"

"I've never lived in the country, but I love walking and things like that."

"How are you with dogs?"

"I love dogs. I wanted one but Tony refused. I often wondered if he might not have wanted one in case it got fond of me and bit him. I've only got the cat because it was my parent's cat."

"Right now, trust Diana with anything. Both of them will help you."

"I can't afford much rent; all the money has gone."

"They don't want any, not for a while anyway. They need the place lived in. To get to it you have to go past their house and their dogs, so they'll know if you have visitors. Diana has a way with dogs, so they'll leave the cat alone. Are you very fond of this car?"

"No, why?"

"Then I'll arrange for you to get another one in the next few days."

Sharon explained to Saul how bad things had become between her and Tony and how he had been violent and had then taken all the money out of their joint bank account. She told him that he would check her phone after she had been out.

"I'll arrange another phone. There is a house phone there. I have the number, use that."

"Thanks, I'll switch mine off. I told Superintendent Evans everything. He was very understanding. All my uniform and kit are at my station, I must get them back."

"Already sorted. You, I and Superintendent Evans and one or two others will get it tomorrow. I need you in civvies. Report to my office in the morning and we'll sort it all then. There you will be seeing the force medical officer and have photos taken, OK? In due course I will arrange for a new solicitor for you, and someone else is taking over Reuben's case and any other cases you have. It looks as if no one is following, so pull away. You may have noticed I've disconnected your sat nav. Just in case anyone should break into your car and steal it."

"Yes, I had noticed. I found Tony going through it recently to see where I had been."

They arrived in convoy with the van at the farm where several dogs ran out to the front and surrounded the car. Sharon looked at them and said, "That is a very big dog!"

"That's Hercules. He's bonkers. He's my brothers' dog. They are very alike, my brother and his dog. Big, noisy, and gentle! Come and meet them. They'll like you."

Jake was coming out of the house as they got out. He said, "Saul you reprobate! Good to see you. It's all right, young lady, the dogs won't hurt you. Come on in, have a drink."

Saul declined. explaining about the dentist. He then said, "Jacob, may I introduce you to WPC Sharon Wright. Her policeman partner was knocking her around."

"Well, he won't be a policeman long. Welcome, Sharon, come on in. The cottage is all ready for you. Saul knows we will help if we can, Sharon."

"Is it all right if I keep my cat at this cottage?"

"Keep a dozen if you like, what is it?" Jake peered into the backseat of the car. "Let's see, oh, a seal point Siamese; I like them. I spent some time in Thailand and met some real nice cats there. Don't look so scared, child. You're safe here and very welcome. Diana, take Sharon inside."

Diana, who had joined them, said, "Yes, come on in. You can tell me all about it if you want, or not if you don't want. I don't know what you eat. I put some supplies in the cottage, but we have a good meal ready now. Saul and you two gentlemen, will you join us?"

"Yes, but I must phone Anna, and Alan. I come bearing messages. Go on in, Sharon, I'll join you soon. Give us your car keys, we'll unload the car and van for you."

Once inside the massive farmhouse kitchen Sharon sat down at the table and said to Diana, "Thank you so much. I never expected such kindness. I've been such a fool and made some dreadful mistakes. Mr Catchpole has been so kind, he rescued me."

"Yes, he did that for me once. Unless you needed help and protection, he wouldn't have brought you here and if he didn't think you were worth it, he wouldn't have either. Don't worry about the dogs, they'll protect you. They are just finding out who you are. They can tell you're distressed, but don't let Hercules dribble on you. He does, that but only to people he likes!"

While Sharon and Diana were talking in the farmhouse, Jake, Saul, and the two officers drove the car and van down to a pretty cottage near the back of the farm buildings. As they unloaded everything, Saul told Jake what the score was and they got the house ready for occupation, returning to the farmhouse about half an hour later. Everyone sat at the table and Diana dished up a splendid meal for all of them.

Saul said, "Jake, Di, Alan wants you to come to his wedding."

"Love to. How is Anna?"

"Fine, can I ring her?"

"She rang earlier. I said I was expecting you. Now, officers would you like anything else to eat?"

Saul said, "Sharon, I'm taking your car back now. Tomorrow, Diana will bring you in to my office in hers. We'll find you another car to use. I don't trust that your car is safe for you. Tell Diana what kind of car you want and she'll get it for you. Now, I'm heading back, do you want me to tell anyone you are safe?"

"Only Gladys. Could I ring her from here?"

Diana took her to the hall and said, "Ring her. When you get to the cottage you have an extension to this phone. For any outside line, dial nine first. Come to us for breakfast."

Back in the kitchen, Saul said, "What I want to know, little brother, is how you and Diana stay so fit when you eat like this?"

"We take a lot of exercise, but less of that, Saul. You are, I think, dealing with those four bodies in the timber yard?"

"Yes, I am."

Diana chipped in, "I think I might be able to help you. I've been working for my old firm. I'll see you tomorrow and tell you what I know."

"I thought you had retired?"

"It's one of the several small jobs I do from time to time."

"I think I'll be busy first thing. Can you see me when Sharon is due to come home? Jake, are you playing this game too?"

"Sort of."

Saul, having driven Sharon's car back to a secure police garage and arranged for it to be thoroughly checked over, then collected his own car, drove it home, took two more pain killers and finally fell, utterly exhausted, into bed.

Chapter 4

Diana walked down to the cottage with Sharon and showed her round. Sharon was delighted. It was warm, comfortable, and peaceful.

Her television had been plugged in and the kitchen cupboards were full of food, as was the fridge. She turned to Diana and said, "What do I owe you?"

"Nothing, dear. We want to help. I like your cat; he seems quite at home."

"Yes, his name is Mung. I think he's glad to be away from Tony. I must pay you some rent, it wouldn't be right not to."

"When you're back on your feet, all right, but until then, no, because we just want it lived in. First, though, I must tell you we have two workers here. One is Nick, the shepherd, who you can trust totally, and John, who you can also trust. All you have to do if you're worried is pick up the phone and dial zero. Is there anything else you need?"

"The only thing I can think of, that I can get tomorrow, is an alarm clock. Tony smashed mine, before I left."

"I'll give you a ring about seven then."

As Sharon was getting into bed later, she remembered that her phone had an alarm on it and turned to set it. There was a text on it that she read. It was not from a number she recognised. She read it.

Bitch u stitched him up. Can u b happy with that? Watch out. He will find you. Don't cum back 2 work

She stared at the phone for some time and then decided to get some sleep, which she found hard. She cried a bit, got a drink of water, cried a lot more and finally drifted off to sleep.

The phone alarm woke her just before seven and, as she got downstairs, Diana rang. She fed the cat and got her things together and headed towards the main house. Already she could see activity in the barns. There was machinery running and a middle-aged man came out of a door and said, "'Morning! You must be Miss Wright. Jake told me you was stopping. I'm John, the cowman. Do you want some milk? I'll drop a small kit off to your porch when I've done. Go on in, they's up. You's a cat, I'm told. We could do with one round here to catch the mice in the feed store."

He smiled at her and went back into the barn. She went to the house and knocked tentatively at the kitchen door and heard Jake bellow, "Come on in, door's open. Morning, sleep well"?

"Not very, I was a bit upset. I feel better now."

"Troubled night?

"Yes, it took ages to calm my mind. I also had a rather nasty text on my phone, probably from a mate of Tony's."

Diana read the message and said, "Let me have the phone, I can probably trace that. I'm coming into town today; I have a job to go to. Saul needs to see this. Here, I have a spare phone, put what numbers you need into it. I have charged it. The charger is with it. My number and Saul's are already on it, and I put Superintendent Evans' number on there as well."

Sharon looked at Diana, who was not dressed very smartly and wondered, "What job do you do if you are so well off?"

"I'm a cleaner just at the moment. It keeps life interesting, well, no, it's very boring, I'm doing it to find out something."

"Yes, Mr Catchpole said you did something else. I suspect rather important to national security?"

"He said you were bright, you are. Do you know him well?"

"No, I only met him yesterday. I know of him, of course, most of the force are scared to death of him, but he has been very kind to me, even when I mucked up big time."

"Yes, I know. He can be very tough but always fair. He does have a bit of a temper, I suspect to go with his red hair. It's a family trait, I think."

"Is there anything else I should know about him, like what to avoid?"

"He's Jewish, so don't offer him pork and avoid any sexist, racist or bigoted opinions around him. It's almost time to leave, what car would you like?"

"I can't afford much of a car, I have no money, I always wanted an estate. "

She watched Jake as he ate a large mouthful of bacon, and then saw Hercules sneaking a sausage off Diana's plate when she wasn't looking. Jake burst into laughter and said, "Dogs one Diana nil. No, lass, I was born Jewish but don't follow it anymore."

Sharon laughed at the look on Diana's face and suddenly felt a huge sense of relief.

Diana looked at her and said, "When was the last time you had a good laugh?"

"It has been ages. One day I'll have a dog of my own. I'd like a collie like your beautiful ones. I've just had a thought, I hate red cars, don't know why."

Diana had a think summing up what Sharon needed and pointed out the car she had needed to be in no way connected to Tony. She told Sharon that nothing should be traceable to her and that the new car would be registered to another address. Sharon pointed out that Tony still had a set of keys to her car and they were joint owners of the house.

Diana told her that would all be sorted out in time and not to worry about it, and then said, "Saul will get your spare keys back. Right, it's almost time to go. All ready? Looking forward to being a murder squad detective?"

"No, terrified, I might muck up again."

"I doubt it. I found it much easier than normal shift work."

"You were on a murder squad?"

"Yes, for a few years, long time ago though."

Sharon was rather overawed when she went into the murder squad office with Jake. He was obviously known there, and said to Alan Withers, "Hello, young Mowgli, is Bagheera in yet?"

"Yes, he's on the phone. I expect at some time someone will tell me what was going on yesterday. Are you and Di coming to our wedding?"

"Love to. What do you want as a wedding present, something built for your house, new doors, furniture?"

"I'll ask, and could we buy some exotic orchids for one of our greenhouses?"

"So, you are going ahead with it?"

"I put the offer in yesterday. I'm waiting to find out."

Alan turned to Sharon, shook her hand and said, "Hello, you must be Sharon Wright. Mr Catchpole said you would be joining us. This here will be your desk; you'll be working with DC Pellow for a while. I've sorted out a locker for you, a car pass for the car park and a permanent issue radio. Welcome to the squad, any problems come to DC Pellow, me, or the guv'nor."

"Thank you, sir. Mr Withers isn't it?"

"That's me. Now, Mr Catchpole says he wants you with him this morning, but normally Julia will look after you. While you're waiting, read the standing orders we have, its already on your desk. Jake, have you time for a coffee? I could murder one."

"No, thanks, Alan, but I expect young Sharon might."

"I'll make it, sir,"

Jake left, and Alan took Sharon over to the kitchen area and said, "Everyone will be coming in. There is the coffee board, how they take it, and you fill in how you like yours."

"Where do I put my kitty money?"

"You'll fit in well, I can tell. I collect it once a month, but the first month is free anyway. We have a lottery fund and a sweepstake, if you want to join. This is Fred Dunlop and Nita, they're our office managers. Now coming in is DS Bickerstaff and behind him DS Paul Christie. The others will introduce themselves."

Sharon was busy for the next fifteen minutes dishing out coffees and teas as the squad members introduced themselves. She was amazed at how friendly everyone was and that she even had her own desk. She had read the book of standing orders and was finding all sorts of interesting things in the desk drawers when Saul came into the office. She jumped up and made him a coffee. He smiled at her and said to Alan, "Do we have any pain killers?"

"In the first aid cupboard, sir, teeth still hurting?"

"Just a bit. Now, bring me up to date."

"OK, Diana rang, she's coming in to see you later, probably late afternoon. I have to go down to Hertfordshire with Paul. I've briefed Geoff and left a list of things you may want to know on my desk. I'm off unless you need me?"

Saul said, "I'll be with you in a little while, Sharon," and went back to his office, via the first aid cabinet.

Geoff called for silence and said, "This is WPC Wright, on attachment, but it's her first time so be gentle with her. Welcome, Sharon." He then allocated a huge number of enquiries to be done and gradually the office emptied of all but a few officers. A woman came in and over to Sharon, "Hello, I'm Julia Pellow. I think I'm lucky enough to have you as my partner. Believe me, you're most welcome. We usually work in pairs but since our last aide left, I've been on my own. I'll show you the ropes, we do things differently here." She was explaining the many things in Sharon's desk, when Saul called them into his office.

He asked, "How are you feeling today, a bit better?"

"Yes, sir, and a great deal calmer, thank you."

"Right, first you see the police surgeon and then the photographer. Julia, go with her."

The police surgeon examined Sharon, asked a lot of questions and recorded the many bruises that had been given to her by Tony, and then they were photographed. They returned to the squad room.

Saul met them, and said, "Now, we're going to your station, for any paperwork, and locker contents. Before we go through your paperwork, is there anything awful in there, any howlers? I had better know now. Julia, if there is, can you help her sort them out?"

"Only one, sir, an accident I dealt with. It's been hanging round for ages. I am waiting for the vehicle examiners report."

"Who did it?"

"Unfortunately, Tony. I have asked him for it many times. He did do it, I know, but I think he is trying to make trouble for me with it. Everything else I have done as far as I can."

"Anything else outstanding?"

"Only a rather difficult burglary, again I'm waiting forensic results."

"Just so long as I know. Nothing in your locker I shouldn't see?"

"I don't think so, the usual women's things, that's all, and my old pocketbooks."

"Julia can help you with them. I have two teenage daughters so I doubt I will be shocked."

"Sir, my shift is on duty there."

"Good, I had hoped they would be. They have been told that you will not be back there, that is all. I'll do the talking but do as I say."

Two streets down from Sharon's station they met Wally and four other members of his department, all above the rank of inspector. They drove in convoy and parked in the front car parking area.

Together they swept into the station and went to the parade room. There were two PCs sitting at a table, apparently playing cards. Then Sharon's shift sergeant and her inspector were fetched, and Wally said, "Wpc Wright is no longer stationed here. I have come with her to clear her desk and locker. Inspector, take me to where she keeps her paperwork and any correspondence relating in any way to her."

"It's all right, I'll fetch it here for you."

"No, you will not. I wish to see it now."

A chief inspector who had come with them said, "Sergeant, please accompany me to WPC Wright's locker."

"I can bring what is in it to you, sir, save you the bother."

"No. I don't think so. It is inappropriate for a man to empty a women's locker. What is in it you do not wish me to see, Sergeant Toller?"

"Nothing, sir, I mean I don't know."

"Which means you do know what is in it! WPC Wright, you have your key? Come on."

"I can assure you, sir, there is nothing much in there."

"You shouldn't even know. Constable, find me a bag, box or something."

In the locker room Sharon went to her locker, put the key in the lock and opened the door. She jumped back as a cascade of rubbish, tin cans and foul-smelling mess fell out. Saul, who was with them, said, "Sharon was this here yesterday?"

"No, sir, it was not."

"Has this happened before?"

"Several times. I am sorry, I should have told you before. I did tell Superintendent Evans. It usually happens after I've had a row with Tony."

"Who has access to the spare key?"

"Sergeant Toller, sir."

The chief inspector said, "That is you, I think. Yes, I thought so. Anything damaged or soiled will be replaced by you out of your own pocket. If you did not put it there you know who did and aided them to do so. How dare you treat a colleague like this, especially one of your own charges? Sharon, what's in there that you need or want?"

"Quite a bit; all my safety equipment, my utility belt, some court shoes, spare tights, socks, clean shirt, some make up, personal things, a pair of riot boots. The rest I will throw away. My old pocketbooks are in a bag in the bottom, a plastic one, because I don't want them soiled."

The PC came back into the room with some binbags and a cardboard box and handed them to Sergeant Toller, who whispered something to him, and both the PCs left the room. The chief inspector, having peered into the locker said, "Right leave the uniform, it will be cleaned or replaced. As will the utility belt. The shoes and boots will be cleaned and delivered spotless to my office by tomorrow. WPC Wright, take what you cannot replace, and the pocketbooks. Sergeant you may now clear the locker."

"I'll just get some gloves…"

"No, you will not. Do it now and I will watch to see you do it properly. Do you admit doing this?"

"I was not alone, sir,"

"But you were in charge. Then do as I say. Ah, Mr Evans, have you got the necessary paperwork? Here is what we have found in the officer's locker. I have informed the Sergeant Toller here that he will be billed for the police equipment that has been damaged or soiled. The rest he will replace. Now I think the superintendent wishes to examine your paperwork and locker. We will remain until that is done. WPC Wright, do you wish to say anything and have you all that you need?"

"I have everything I need. I think it would be wiser not to say what I think."

"Then go with Miss Pellow and Mr Catchpole. I will list everything and get replaced anything you wish to have. I will forward a copy of the list to the squad office for you,"

Sharon left the room and was obviously upset. Julia ushered her into an office and calmed her down. As they left to go down the corridor leading to the back door of the station, Saul joined them, and said, "Julia, please fetch the car round the back, so we can load in the things we are taking. Here are the keys. I'll meet you out there. You, PC Brown, can you help me please?"

Neville Brown came up to Sharon and said, "Sharon, are you Ok, can I help?"

"No, it's all right, Nev, I'll be fine, just look out for yourself?"

"I'll tell Helen you're ok then. She was worried about you. Sir, thank you for your assistance yesterday."

"Should you be back on duty so soon, you can hardly go out with those two shiners?"

"I am just jailer for today, the shift was very short. Sharon, thanks for what you brought me."

"PC Brown, are you happy on this shift?"

The pause before he answered told Saul everything.

"Yes, sir, I suppose so."

"Would you rather move to another station?"

"Honestly, yes, sir, it is not at all what I expected."

Sharon walked out of the backdoor into the yard as Julia drove in and parked their car by the back door. Together they put several bags and boxes of Sharon's things into the boot. Julia said, "How long have you been putting up with that kind of thing?"

"Since Tony wanted me to leave the job, and I wouldn't. I did complain to Inspector Pollock. He said it was only horseplay and not to make a fuss. It got worse after that, he told Tony I had complained. There wasn't anyone I could trust. Sergeant Toller and Tony are best mates, they go drinking together and between them they have turned almost everyone on the shift against us women."

"Is there no one on your shift who you can trust?"

"Helen Pickering, they have been doing it to her as well, Sergeant Toller hates women in the job. He was really nasty when she got her tutors course, and Nev was attached to her. Nev is nice, he hasn't been corrupted yet. The other officer that is OK is Malcolm Austin. He's on leave at the moment. He's a beat officer who has helped us and he complained too. Since then he has had every shitty job going, unless we got it first. On nights, we're the only four who actually do any work. The others play cards and watch porn videos in the canteen all night."

"Anyone else you like?"

"The custody sergeant, Les Pike, the jailer, Mick Pantin."

"Right, get in the car. Ah, here comes the guv'nor."

As Saul walked towards the car a large plastic bag fell from an upstairs widow and splashed its contents all over him. The contents looked like and smelled of urine. Saul was drenched, as was the front of the car, but the two women had got into the car before it hit him. Saul looked up and heard male laughter coming from the window concerned. Saul did not take very kindly to being doused with stale urine. Already angry, he moved at incredible speed back into the building and sprinted up the stairs, passing Wally and several other officers from the complaints and discipline team. They followed him to see what he was running to. He pushed open the door to the gent's toilet and shower room and found the two PCs who had been in the parade room laughing, hiding behind one of the cubicle doors.

"Explain yourselves!"

"It wasn't meant for you, mate, it was for the two split arses. The skipper said to chuck it because the station was being searched. Sorry, mate."

"One, I am *not* your mate. Two, I am Detective Chief Superintendent Catchpole. Three, you have just made a very serious mistake!"

Wally and the rest of his team had heard this as they joined them and the two men were told to stand to attention. Very few had ever seen Saul at his angriest. He told the two men exactly what he thought of them, what he thought of their behaviour, their appearance, their intelligence, and their lack of future prospects. He doubted their judgment and informed them they would be paying for the cleaning of all his attire and the car and yard. This angry tirade lasted some time and not once did he repeat himself. Wally winced and the rest of the team just stood amazed, rather gratified at what was said. Saul, having finally paused for breath, continued to say, "If you ever use that offensive term for any female again, I will see to it that you suffer for it. Be thankful you are not now on the way to casualty. I will leave it with you, Wally, and I want a public apology from them to me, and the two ladies who they were aiming at. I am speaking to the chief about this and

I expect you are. Yes, I thought so. Get them out of my sight while I try and wash some of this off."

Putting his jacket in a bin bag, he cleaned himself as best he could, then went out to the car in the yard put the bin bag in the boot and said, "Julia, please will you drive? I am just too angry. Thank you for washing the windscreen and the front of the car."

"Sharon did that, sir."

Once Saul was sitting in the front passenger seat, he noticed the windows were already wound down.

"I apologize to both of you, on behalf of the force and every decent man. How many women have resigned from this station since Toller has been here?"

"I think it is eleven in the last three years. I would have gone but the more they tried to make me go, the more determined I was to stick it out."

"Good for you. I must go and change. I have a spare outfit at the office. No, I took it to be cleaned last week and was due to pick it up today. We have to go almost past my house, so come and have a coffee while I get some fresh clothes. I know you know my wife, don't you, Julia?"

"Yes. Er, sir, are those two PCs still in one piece?"

"Unfortunately, yes."

"We heard everything. So did most of the neighbourhood. I have never seen you that angry before, ever."

"Did I go over the top?"

"Not that I thought. It was wonderful! You have a remarkable vocabulary. I didn't know there were that many derogatory adjectives."

"I don't remember swearing, did I?"

"Not once. I hope I can remember it all."

"Please, don't!"

"Oh, I think it's essential. We need it for the cartoons on the office wall."

Julia and Sharon then repeated almost word for word what Saul had said, and Saul groaned and pleaded, "Oh no, please stop."

"Actually, I think the first bit was best, where you introduced the comment of 'the mentality of a baboon, the manners of a warthog, the subtlety of a rhino, and the sliminess of a worm', and then there was the bit about them being likened to a 'mentally deficient amoeba'?"

"I didn't say that, did I?"

"Yes, you did, here I think this is your house, sir?"

"Can I bribe you two to silence with a coffee and some lunch?"

"No, but we will come in anyway. Just to warn you, sir, I think that chief inspector had a camera on, so it will be recorded somewhere."

"Please don't tell my wife and daughters what I said."

"All right. Sir, you still look very flushed."

"Very funny! That happens when I lose my temper. I'll have a shower, get changed and be as quick as I can. I am sorry, ladies, if I embarrassed you."

"Well, you didn't embarrass me, I really enjoyed it. I needed something to cheer me up!"

"Me too sir, I think this will go down in the annals of murder squad history. I wonder how Tarik – he's the cartoonist, Sharon – will portray mentally deficient amoeba."

"Enough, the pair of you! I submit. I lost my temper and now I shall have to apologise to them."

"Don't you dare, sir! If they were who I think they were, everything you said is true. Some of the tricks they played were awful, crude, rude and very insulting. Toller encouraged them, even suggested some. If you know how many times I was told I only had two uses, one in the bedroom, the other in a kitchen, and to go and make the tea for them, you'd not retract a word of it."

Saul let himself in to his hallway, called his wife and introduced Sharon. Anna looked at him, sniffed the air and said, "I don't know what you got covered in but go and wash, dear. Hello, Julia, come on in. I'll get something to eat. Sharon, welcome and sit down and tell me all about it!"

From halfway up the stairs a voice called," Don't you dare, ladies."

Very briefly, Julia explained what had happened. Anna laughed and said, "I think that is worse than the time he came home covered in elephant dung. I take it he had a bit to say about it?"

"Yes, rather a lot, but we are sworn to secrecy."

"That bad, eh? Best leave him to calm down then. Do you take sugar, Sharon?

"No, thank you, Mrs Catchpole,"

"I understand you're staying with my sister-in-law?"

"Yes, I am."

"Tell her the whole story, she'll love it, I do like Diana. She fell foul of Saul once, but got the better of him. It was very good for him. He is so senior, has been for ages, that he seldom gets challenged these days. Don't look so worried, he'll see the funny side of it soon."

When Saul came down later, clean and washed and in a different suit he smiled and said, "That is much better. Oh, this looks like a good meal, yes, please."

He ate some sandwiches, had a cup of tea and then said, "Come on, ladies, work calls."

Anna said, "Must you dash off?"

"I'm afraid so; we have a lot to do and once again I'll be late home."

"You always are when these cases start up. How's your toothache?"

"Better, thanks."

They drove back to the murder squad office in comparative silence.

Chapter 5

Once back at the squad, office Sharon and Julia went out on enquires. Saul read through the immediate messages and Alan rang to say that the Stevens family had been positively identified as those at the wood yard, and he was staying over for the night to do follow up enquiries there. Meanwhile, Saul retreated to his office and went through all the messages and completed enquiries.

By five o'clock the office was full again as everyone had returned. Geoff Bickerstaff popped his head round Saul's door and said the squad were ready for a briefing. Saul knew, the moment he went into the general office when the laughter abruptly stopped, that someone had told them of the events of the morning. Julia smiled sweetly with a very mischievous grin, and Sharon looked a little guilty.

Saul called for a briefing by saying, "All right, you had better hear it from the horse's mouth. I lost my rag and got a bit verbose. This does not mean however, that you can either use what I said, or take the mickey. Now, we have found out a lot. These bodies are the Stevens family. Dental records can prove it. They hired a car because they only had a small one and they were coming on holiday. He was a banker, apparently very respectable and his wife a housewife who helped out at adult literacy classes some evenings as she had been a teacher. We know little about the children as yet, expect that the boy, Jason was clever, curious and observant. They were Mr and Mrs Ordinary, no convictions, not even motoring ones and about as law abiding as you can get. Yes, Simon?"

"What kind of banking?"

"High street, deputy manager. Worked his way up from leaving school. His wife was very small, only about four foot three. There is nothing we know yet that gives us any clues about their lifestyle."

"Had they been to this area before?"

"Never. Their previous holidays were in Devon, Bournemouth and the Isle of Wight. What we do know is the boy was computer mad and used to go on the internet a lot."

"So, if they were so law abiding why get killed? Did they come across something or see something?"

"Yes, Paul, we have to consider it. They left Harrogate on the sixteenth. They were booked in at the Falcon Inn on the seventeenth but didn't turn up. It looks like they didn't die for another couple of days, which was over the weekend. Where were they and their car then? Yes, Tarik?"

"The car had been there we think since the sixteenth according to dog walkers. The agricultural merchants nearby saw a family there on that afternoon. They describe them quite well, said the woman was tiny. We are still looking at the car. The police support teams are still searching."

"Any more on the cellar, Fred?"

"Yes. They think their DNA is there but there is more. Several DNA traces from different people. There is some blood type B, but this family, so I understand, were all O. The lab also says there are signs of cocaine and something else they are trying to identify. Some of the samples have been there some time, we think. We also found some scraps of film exposed; the lab says 35 mm So far, we have yet to find anywhere that the key we found in Bill Birtwhistle's car fits, but someone suggested it looked like a key for a caravan, so we are following that up. We have got a couple of fingerprints from the trolley in the woodyard that the manager said had been moved. They are going off to be checked now. When we have finished here this afternoon, I want to search the yard again and the surrounding scrubland, with heat seeking gear and dogs, cadaver dogs. I have a bad feeling about this. What if they saw something, there at the yard, that meant they had to die?"

"Like what?"

'I don't know. I've done a check of missing persons; kids between seven and fourteen. There are rather a lot and all of them, bar a few, have been using chat rooms on the net before going missing. I rang Alan and he is getting the computers at the Stevens' house checked. Hertfordshire are being very helpful."

"Have we found the travellers' site yet?"

"Yes, but they have gone. We found the same kind of firewood there. We are going now to ask all the locals what they the know."

"Sir, did Reuben get released?"

"No, Sharon, he didn't. He is due in court tomorrow morning. We have identified him. His real name is Derek Thomas and he has multiple convictions, mainly for dishonesty and drugs, but a couple for ABH. Anything else? Yes, Simon."

"I got nosy about Bill Birtwhistle. I spoke to the people who live nearby. He spends very little time at his room and goes out a lot. The newsagent told me he regularly buys porn magazines. It's funny we didn't find any in his room."

"So, he has somewhere else. We need to find it."

The briefing broke up; some officers going off duty, others going out on more enquiries. Sharon and Julia wrote up their enquiries and just as they were finishing, Diana was shown in. Saul was busy on the phone, so Diana came and sat with Sharon and said, "I got that number traced. Shall I tell you or Saul?

"Mr Catchpole, please"

"Meanwhile I got you another car. I hope you like it, I'll hang on and cadge a lift home with you, if I may?"

"I may be a while, I'm not sure if they need me to stay on. Mr Catchpole gave me these sets of keys to the other car."

Saul came into the main office and said, "Diana, please come on through."

Diana looked him up and down and said, "New suit, Saul, not seen that one before?"

"No, I do have several you know."

There were muffed giggles from several in the room. Saul smiled wryly and said, "Shut up you lot, it's not that funny!"

As soon as he had shut the door in the main office, he heard howls of laughter coming from it. Diana looked at him and said, "Not elephants again?"

"Worse. Now, what can you tell me?"

"Several things. Sharon got this message on her phone last night. I got a friend to trace it. Find whoever has that number and you have your man."

"What else can you tell me?"

"Are these bodies you found connected with a group of travellers?"

"We're not sure, possibly."

"Well, if they are, you're not the only ones interested in these travellers. Some of them are not what they seem."

"Tell me."

"You know, there is an old tale that gypsies steal children. Not true of course, but several children have gone missing when this particular group have been in the area. From all over the country. We need your DC to back off. He has already made the connection and this group is already under observation."

"Are they connected to the bodies in the timber yard?"

"Yes and no. One of the men working at the yard, a William Birtwhistle, was in the same cell as one of the travellers, some years back. Both of them did a computer course while they were inside. Now this traveller we know goes on the net a lot, chat rooms and the like. Calls himself Midsummer. We haven't caught him doing anything unlawful, yet, but we are watching him. Now he met Birtwhistle several times last month at a pub called the Tempest Arms at Elslack. They exchanged what looked like photos or documents in a large envelope. They seemed to know each other rather well."

"Can you be more specific?"

"Not at the moment, no. I'll talk to someone who may talk to you. We do suspect that somewhere they have been holding some of these missing children, all boys, by the way, and then the boys disappear. We think it's a big gang of paedophiles."

"Any thoughts as to what this family, who we have identified, have to do with it?"

"Check the child out. Where did they come from?"

"Hitchin."

"This group were in Milton Keynes for a while, recently."

"Do you know where they are now?"

"Yes, try Cross Hills, on the Colne road. About ten in the morning. Our person won't be there."

"Do you know of a Reuben in that group?"

"Yes, quite a clever artist, horrid man but clever. No, I don't think it's him. He has a rather talented sculptress girlfriend, called Petunia."

"Any idea where this Birtwhistle might have a caravan?

"Yes. Go up the lane past The Tempest, up to a forest at the top of the road. Deep in the woods, have a look. Mind you, it's impossible to get to it unseen during the day. Not easy at night. It's well hidden but there is a way up the stream nearby."

"Will it upset your lot if we raid it?"

"Not at all, but he will see you coming."

"Can you show us?"

"No, I don't want him seeing me."

"Do any of this group or him have a 9mm gun?"

"Not that I know of, but I wouldn't be surprised."

"Thanks. I'll keep your lot informed."

"No problem, I like Sharon, she reminds me very much of myself at her age."

"In what way?"

"She has guts and brains and is very observant and can join the dots together. Be careful, I might just recruit her."

"I take it Jake and you are working on this, I thought you had retired."

"Correct."

"Can you suggest what we should do now?"

"Just because someone has no convictions don't rule them out, especially the female of the species."

"The Stevens woman?"

" No, you clot; look closer, look for the wood in the trees, the fallen and sawn up trees."

"How do you know that?"

"I buy firewood there sometimes."

"When were you last there?"

"About the time the travellers were last there, about six weeks ago. They bought a fiver's worth of logs then."

"Anything else?"

"Things are not always what they seem. If that man, Bill, is Mrs Moreby's son, she must have had him when she was seven. People are not always who they say they are."

"I'll check, thanks,"

"Saul, I'll help look after Sharon, but from what she told me, you seem to have a barrel full of rotten apples. Are you sorting it?"

"Yes. That's why I had to change my clothes earlier today."

"I'll find out, I usually do. My love to Anna. I'll wait for Sharon. I doubt she slept much last night."

They went into the main squad office and Saul said, "Okay, Sharon, Julia, knock off for today please. Sharon, Diana needs a lift home."

As Sharon and Diana got outside, Diana handed Sharon a set of car keys and said, "I hope you're pleased with it; I have a friend in the trade who owed me a favour. Here we are."

Sharon looked at the car they had stopped by. All she could see was a dark blue, rather smart Subaru estate.

"I can't afford that!"

"It was a straight swap for your car, I promise. Your car is being examined at the moment, at HQ. They will pick it up in a day or so. This one is covered on my insurance, as are you to drive it."

"How can I ever repay you?"

"By remaining strong and getting your life back on track. I need you to promise me something, "

"If I can."

"If you need to talk, day or night, you'll come to me. Don't cry on your own, unless you want to. Come on, take us home."

Saul went to another part of the building to see Wally at his office. Wally Evans looked up, smiled and said, "I was coming to see you. I'd have come earlier but I wasn't sure how long it would take you to calm down."

"Don't rub it in! I'll have to apologise, I know. They made me see red."

"Don't do anything of the sort. You were magnificent. What I, and my team, have found out today beggars belief. The chief wants to see us in half an hour.

I'll tell you what we found out. Now, the other WPC on the shift has confirmed what we were told. Her locker had also been filled with rubbish. Those two little creeps that upset you so are totally unpleasant and we found all sorts of things in their lockers. Files, most of which are a gross neglect of duty. Toller is even worse. We've been through the correspondence register. He's lost all sorts of important documents including some vital stuff. In his locker we found files years old, that he had marked up as having gone back to either the Crown Prosecution Service or the originator. There was a vehicle examination report done by Gilchrist, that WPC Wright had been asking for. We looked at everything in the station, it took us all day, and I had to call in some more of my department. It will take weeks to go through it all. It looks as though Toller had deliberately trashed anything the women officers put through him, then we went to his house, and found a load more, including an unexplained very large amount of money, cash."

"Go on."

"You remember that robbery at the Bradford and Bingley, what six weeks ago?"

"I do. They got away with a lot, somehow they slipped through our cordon."

"That's the one. The notes were all marked with an invisible dye and were to go back to the Bank of England to be taken out of circulation. We found £30,000 of it at Toller's place. We checked and he and his shift were on duty as part of the cordon. We have, therefore, nicked him. He lives alone but we found several phones and we're checking the calls on them. One of the creeps who upset you has decided to talk. He admits helping get the robbers through the cordon. Toller actually took the men out of the area in a police vehicle. Rose, this creep, has also admitted having a backhander for his silence about it. The inspector is in on it too."

"The whole shift is corrupt?"

"No, not all of them. The two women officers and another male beat officer were not and were left well alone, and they were trying very hard to get rid of them. Gilchrist is one of the gang. It seems that all in the gang were on the payroll of some serious villains, we have yet to find out who."

"What about further up the chain of command?"

"Not sure. We're investigating."

"Why has nothing been spotted before?

"That's what worries me and the chief."

"Have you found anything against Sharon Wright?"

"No, except what Toller and the others have been trying to dump on her. The chief wants a debrief and you're to be there too."

"Wally, I did go OTT with those two. I've been told what I said. I'll have to retract some of it."

"Don't. I doubt anyone will forget it or want to anger you that much for a while. It's very useful to me, if you must know. I need someone who can put the fear of God into the ranks, without uttering one obscenity or swear word."

"Wally, did I really liken them to baboons?"

"Yes, and a lot of other animals. I wish I had your zoological knowledge."

"Amoeba too?"

"Yes, and worms, rhinos and my favourite, natural khaki. Good phrase that, I might use it."

"What have I done? Do you have Toller's telephone numbers?"

"Yes."

"Is this one of them?"

"Yes, it is."

Saul explained about the text message and then said, "What about Gilchrist, is he out yet?"

"Bailed this afternoon, he's been suspended and warned not to contact her."

"Did he admit anything?"

"Like all bullies, when he realised the deep poo was in, he folded and sang like a bird. He refused the breathalyser though. It's time to go to see the chief. This should be interesting, to say the least."

"I will apologise to him."

"If you must."

The chief constable, who was relatively new in his post, having come from another force when his predecessor retired, had a large and comfortable office. There were several chairs that were set out ready for a meeting. As Saul and Wally came in, he looked up, saw them and chuckled.

"I'll be putting you forward for some talks to various organisations, the Literary Society, the Zoological Institute, the Oxford Dictionary. I found this in my in tray just now, it is really rather good!".

He handed Saul a complete transcript of his outburst followed by the quotation, 'Saul, Saul, why persecutest thou me, 'Acts, chapter V."

Saul groaned and said, "I am sorry, sir. I'll make a public apology if you wish it. I lost my temper, that's the long and the short of it."

"You'll do no such thing! I will accept your apology, yes, and tell you that senior officers should not lose control, but that's as far as it goes. Really, Saul, I know the provocation was great, but normally you would have risen above it. Have you any excuse?"

"No excuse, no. I did have raging toothache."

"Have you still?"

"Not as bad as it was, but yes."

"Then sit down and tell me how I rid myself of the hornets' nest you have stirred up. Er, I don't think you have covered hornets; we shall have to add it to the list."

Saul winced. He knew that every animal joke would be cracked at his expense over the next weeks.

"If I hadn't come across a shoplifter on my way back from the dentist and the subsequent assault on an officer by the shoplifter, I would never have known. I was appalled at what I found. What I want to know is how this got so far without someone knowing."

"So would I. I have the commanding officers coming in now, I want an explanation too. It does not solve our immediate problem. When the wheel comes off like this, we will have to act, now. We have to move a lot of personnel and have a complete reshuffle. I have asked the personnel department to join us, they are just arriving. We need to consider suitable replacements in all the ranks and almost find a new shift, if not a new station. We need to put this right. If you have any suggestions, please let me have them. Come in and sit down everybody. Superintendent Evans, can you bring us all up to date please?"

Wally told the whole meeting what they had found and what they needed to clarify and further investigate. Several suggestions for officers to be posted in were made, and then the chief said, "How many officers have you arrested, suspended or want out of your way?

"I have arrested five on that shift. PCs. Rose, Oliver, Corby, Sergeant Toller and Inspector Pollock, and the traffic Sergeant Boniface, who is Gilchrist's supervisor. I am investigating three others on the shift and two other officers elsewhere, and Saul, I am afraid I have also suspended DS Rankin, who I believe was on your squad not long ago."

"That does not surprise me. I never did like the bumptious little toad."

The chief muttered, "That's good. I'll add it to the list."

Saul blushed, but held his tongue. The Chief was obviously enjoying himself. For some time, they discussed the next course of action and officers they thought might be suitable to replace the ones taken off the shift. Then the phone rang and after a short conversation, the chief said, "Wonderful! Now the press has been told something is going on at that station. That's all we need! Right, I've made a decision. I want this kind of corruption and behaviour stamped out, and to do so we need to take aggressive steps, and spot check-ups all through the force. It means a lot of work for all of you. Thank you, Saul, I'll keep you up to date. You have done your share, or should I say the lion's share."

"Thank you, sir, for that gem. I'll go and see if I'm any further with my real job, catching murderers."

"Good idea, oh and Saul, I know you're working like a dog, but please don't take your nose off the scent, or pick up any lame ducks?"

"How droll, sir. I'll try to bring home the bacon."

"Get out!"

Saul returned to his office, checked the progress of the many enquiries, and then rang Diana, and asked if Sharon was all right. Diana said, "Oh yes, she's much happier. In fact, she's telling me a very funny story. She described someone I know having a face like a bulldog chawing on a wasp, when he lost his temper. It seems like she might have let the cat out of the bag."

"Not you, too. I submit, enough."

"Next you'll be playing possum or dead!"

"Goodnight, Diana."

"Goodnight, Bagheera."

Chapter 6

The next morning Saul was up early and headed into his office. His toothache had gone. As he drove, he accepted that he would have to endure animal jokes and had therefore gone in extra early to swerve them. He signed in and then took himself off with his sergeant, Geoff Bickerstaff, to open the inquest on the Stevens family. Once that was done, they returned to an amazingly deserted office, with only Fred Dunlop and Nita in there.

Suspicious, Saul asked, "Okay, Fred, where have they all gone?"

"Some wild goose chase I expect. Or out catching red herrings."

"Well, where are all the cartoons and the jokes. Not up yet?"

"Don't know what you mean, sir."

"Of course you don't."

On his office desk was a book which, when he turned it over, he saw was a bestiary. He smiled and put it on his bookshelf. He remained reading all the statements and files relating to the case until about eleven a.m., when he called Geoff in.

"Geoff, I want to know where Bill Birtwhistle is at the moment. I know where he has a caravan. I need a team to look. It's unlikely we can surprise him there, so we need to know when is out of the way. I think it's in Lancashire, so I have contacted my oppo there and he's happy to help us."

"He's not down the woodyard, none of them are, they can't work there so Mrs Moreby gave them a week's holiday. I'll see if I can find out. Anything else you need?"

"How is WPC Wright doing?"

"Fine. She and Julia seem to work very well as a team. Guv, there are a lot of rumours going around about you, about her and a shift at Main Road…"

"Go on."

"Well, they say she was beaten up by a traffic man and her shift has been arrested, and you caught them doing something, and told them what you thought of them. Just now someone asked me where she was living, when I went up to the canteen."

"Who?"

"Andy Bates, a traffic skipper. We served together on a shift years ago. I never liked him much. I told him I had no idea and asked him what it had to do with him."

"What did he say?"

"That Tony Gilchrist was one of his officers and was really cut up about it and wanted to know. I said that maybe he should ask you."

"Well done. I will tell you, Geoff, I saw Gilchrist beating young Sharon up. She's terrified of him, with good reason. I must admit when I sprayed him with CS gas, when I arrested him, it felt wonderful. I've put her in a safe house. If you need her to come in use this number. Look after her, please."

"I'll do that. She's extremely bright, picks things up real quick."

"She had an excellent record until she was harassed by her shift skipper. Yes, I discovered a right mess at Main Road and yes, I lost my rag. I'm sure you heard about that."

"That was brilliant, if I may say, and if nothing else you have given us something to aim at, a better use of a wider vocabulary. I'll just answer the phone."

He beckoned Saul over and made some notes and then said, "We'd better get the shovels out. The heat sensitive cameras and cadaver dogs have picked up five possible buried bodies in and around the timber yard. Tarik was right."

"He usually is. Anything else?"

"This just came for you."

He handed Saul a sealed envelope and Saul studied the contents.

"That confirms Tarik's suspicions. I'd better get overalls and wellies. We have to do some digging. Is Alan on the way back with Paul yet?"

"On their way, the lab results are due in any time. I'll leave Fred here and come digging too. Shall I call in the support group?"

"If they're not already on their way, yes. Explain to Fred, about Sharon as well, then let's get digging."

Most of the squad arrived at the woodyard quite quickly. The support group of sixty officers were there within the hour. The area was sectioned off and digging began immediately, with scenes of crime officers waiting. One area was inside the yard, in an overgrown scrubby area, behind some stored tree trunks. Two more were in the thicket just outside the yard fence. One was in a culvert by the stream and the last one was just behind the old brick building at the far end of the yard.

They had been digging half an hour when they found the first body. It had been there some time and all that remained was some clothing, some shoes and some skeletal remains. Saul came and looked and then left it to the scenes of crime officers. As he was walking back to the area where he was helping to dig, his phone rang. He answered it, spoke briefly, made two calls and then went in search of Julia and Sharon. He took Sharon aside and said, "Have you told anyone where you are living?"

"No. I don't actually know the address, why?"

"Were you followed yesterday when you and Diana went home?"

"Not that I was aware of."

"Well, someone has been watching the farm. When they were challenged by John, the cowman, they asked if you were staying there; it's all right, he said he had no idea what they were on about and to clear off. He told Diana immediately. There were two men; one came up to the farmhouse and started to ask a lot of questions. Which got him nowhere. Then he made a bad mistake; he tried to intimidate Diana, so Hercules took grave exception to the man and bit him in the backside and chased him off the farm and down the road. Diana got a photo of him and the registration number of the car. He and the other bloke left very fast indeed. Don't worry, Diana and Hercules are fine."

"Who was it? Do you know?"

"Unfortunately, yes. It was Tony and I think a man called Boniface."

"Please tell me it was Tony that got bitten."

"It was. Don't look so delighted."

"Oh, but I am. I've been so careful, I'm sure I wasn't followed."

"So was Diana, which means we have to look at something else. He told Diana that you had something valuable of his and that he wanted it back. Do you know what?"

"I didn't take anything of his, I only took what was mine. I do have my bank book, but last month there was only about £100 in the account. I haven't checked it this week."

"Have you spoken to a solicitor yet?"

" Not yet. What do I do now?"

"Carry on digging. I have arranged for both of them to be arrested. That's happening now, so carry on. You know we've already found one body? It has been there a long time and we think it might be of a child. I'll come back and see you in a bit."

Saul checked all the sites and then made and received some more calls. After a couple of hours nothing else was found so everyone took a break and gathered round the catering wagon. Alan Withers arrived, spoke with Saul and then went off to deal with the press. Detective Sergeant Paul Christie took over from Saul, who drove back to the office. On his way into the car park he noticed two officers looking at Sharon's old car that had been parked outside, ready to be taken away.

He parked and walked up behind them and said, "What are you two doing?"

"Just come out for some air."

"Have you nothing better to do?"

"We're on a course, sir, and we're on a break."

"Which course?"

"Constable Refresher Course, sir"

"Then I'll walk back with you. Why the interest in that car?"

"I've not seen it here before. It's all right, sir, we know our way."

Saul smiled and said, "So do I," and stuck to them like glue as they went to the training area at the back of the building.

One of them said, "I must visit the gents before I go back," and the other said, "Yes so must I."

As Saul was wearing his identification card that was worn by all regular staff at the premises, he knew they were unlikely to confide in him willingly. He waited patiently in the corridor outside the gents and then saw one of the training staff walking towards him.

He said, "Hello, Archie, do you have a Constable Refresher Course running today?"

"No, not for at least two weeks, sir, only course is a probationer course tomorrow."

"Thank you, could you do me a big favour?"

" If I can, certainly,"

"Find out who these two collar numbers are for me, as soon as you can."

Several minutes later the two constables emerged from the gents and looked rather disconcerted to find Saul still there.

"Yes, I am still here. There is no refresher course. Shall we start again. Why are you here?"

"I am sorry, sir. We came here on a correspondence run, we shouldn't have been hanging around."

"I know that. Either give me the truth, PC Martin, or we go up to Superintendent Evans and you can explain to him why you saw fit to lie. That is the falsehood and prevarication clause in our discipline code."

"I was asked to see if that car was here, sir, to see what was in it."

"Who by?"

"PC Gilchrist. He rang me earlier and asked me to."

"Are you aware that he is suspended and you should have no contact with him?"

"No, sir, I wasn't, and had I known that I would have refused. Alf here doesn't know anything about it. He was just with me."

"What were you looking for?"

"He wanted to know if his girlfriend had any luggage in it, specifically her jewellery case. I asked him why he couldn't ask her himself and he said they had had a row."

"And if it had been there what did he want you to do?"

"Ring him and tell him. I only agreed because he said he would give me a good report on a recent attachment I had on traffic. I am sorry I lied, sir, I only did so because he said I mustn't get caught."

"Did you not think it strange"?

"Yes, I did, but I wanted a good report, although I did think it odd that he would be doing an appraisal, not the inspector or sergeant."

"I think you had better come up to my office, both of you and tell me everything you know. The pair of you keep your mouths shut. Do not speak to or have any contact with Gilchrist again."

Saul took them to Wally, and they were most informative, so he left Wally to deal with them, and rang Diana.

"Diana, did you check the Peugeot before you gave it to Sharon?"

"Yes, I did. Nothing in or on it. When you rang earlier, I had a think and I wondered, does Sharon have any jewellery?"

"You're asking me? I don't know."

"Well, I know she has an ingot pendant, it is rather unusual. I noticed it at breakfast yesterday. It has some strange markings on it. If she has it with her, can you take a good look at it?

"What are you saying?

"Somehow, they have traced her, not the car. From what you told me earlier, I wonder what she has or knows that is so important."

"So do I. When you spoke to Gilchrist, how did he explain how he knew where she was?"

"He didn't. He tried to bully and intimidate me. His mistake. John said he had been trespassing, trying to have a good look round. He never got near the cottage because of the dogs. We have, as you know, a huge sign on all the gates saying no trespassing, and guard dogs running free."

"This is getting rather sinister. We know he is crooked, as are his so-called mates, but I wonder what is behind this."

"Something rather big by the sound of it. Incidentally, did you get the envelope? If you want to look at that caravan, do it this afternoon. Bill is visiting the travellers camp today and has gone off somewhere with them. I did a further check. The caravan was reported stolen four years ago and the land it is on is private. The landowner says you have his permission to search and remove anything you see fit. He is a mate of ours. Lord Clark, if you want to know. I was at uni with him."

"Thank you. Yes, I got the envelope and we will act on it."

Soon a combined Lancashire and Yorkshire police team were at the caravan in the woods. The access to it was full of hazards; an area of razor wire, a deep ditch with broken glass at the bottom and several gin traps hidden in the undergrowth. The key that had been found in Bill's car fitted the door and soon they were in. Inside, they found a huge amount of seriously disturbing pornography, a laptop computer, a shelf full of videos and CDs, some correspondence, and a list of telephone numbers. The generator behind the caravan was fingerprinted and when checked was also found to be stolen. Among many items taken from the caravan was a video camera, several sets of handcuffs and rolls of strong parcel tape. Once everything was removed, the scenes of crime officers went in and took swabs. There were traces of blood and seminal fluid. The caravan was also very filthy and when the original owner was contacted, he explained that he had been paid out on the insurance and no longer wanted the caravan. The insurance company did not want it either. It was sealed after a copy of the search warrant was left on the table inside. After a flurry of telephone calls, Bill Birtwhistle was circulated as a wanted person.

Saul returned to the timber yard where three more bodies had already been found, and there were indications that another body was soon to be discovered. He conferred with Paul at the scene and then said, "Are you all right, Paul? You look rather distressed. Let me stay here and get you back and help Alan with the press releases and other stuff."

"It has been rather grizzly, sir, and as you know, I don't have the strongest of stomachs. I must say I was impressed with young Sharon, she found two of the bodies and knew exactly what to do. "

Saul found Sharon and Julia at the catering van.

"Well done, you two. Look, I need to get both of you back to HQ. Something has come up that I need you for."

Julia smiled and said, "I was getting pretty knackered anyway. I never was good at gardening."

They fetched their things and got into Saul's car. As they drove away Sharon said, "I've been thinking about what you said, so I rang the bank to get the balance on my account and it has rather frightened me. I need to talk to you about it."

"Wait until we get back. Don't worry. I'll explain when we get to the office."

It was very late afternoon when they got back to the office. Saul shut the door and said, "Sit down both of you. Sharon, how much have you told Julia?"

"Everything. She has been very understanding."

"Right, get us all a coffee while I just check the messages and then we need to have a good chat."

Ten minutes later they resumed, and he said, "Sharon do you wear any jewellery?"

"Only my pendant, Tony gave it to me when we first moved in together."

"May I see it please?"

"Sure, it is rather difficult to remove, Julia can you help me?"

Julia managed, with some difficulty, to undo the intricate and rather solid fastening, that appeared to have been sealed with some sort of adhesive and handed the pendant to Saul. He looked at it and said, "Are you very fond of it?"

"Not really, not any more. I must tell you; I got my balance from the bank and I think there must be a mistake. It has over £20,000 in there. That can't be right. It went into the account five days ago. It's funny you should want the pendant. It has half a code engraved on it, for the bank account. Neither of us can withdraw more than £500 without that code. Tony said it was as a safety precaution. He has a similar pendant, with his half of the code on it. He asked me for this when I tried to leave. He said that as he gave it to me it was his. Before you got there, he was trying to get it, he tried to pull it off. I thought it was just him being mean."

"No wonder he didn't want you to leave. He had put a huge amount of money into the account and you were going off with his means of getting it back."

"But what I don't understand is that the bank say I paid that money in. They asked for ID. I have not been into the bank for ages, about two or three months. The manager said I had gone in. He got all worried when I said I had not paid any money in; the woman he then described sounds a bit like Alana Colbright, who is one of Tony's girlfriends, or I think mistresses."

Julia said, "She works in the pay department at HQ, I know her, I think she is secretary to the finance officer,"

"Thanks, Julia, this is what we do. First thing in the morning we sort this out with the bank, get you to a solicitor that has no contact with Tony, and I am afraid we need a thorough search of your things, Sharon. Have you any idea where that sort of money may have come from?"

"None. It's scary. How could he get that much?"

"Not legally, I suspect. I need to borrow this pendant. Do you have your own bank account?"

"Yes, one the one my pay goes into. Then it is transferred, apart from a small amount, into the joint account. That I will have to change immediately. I don't want the pendant now, take it."

"Julia, will you please go with her in the morning?"

"Of course, sir. Would you like Sharon to stay with me tonight?"

"I can't, but thanks. I have my cat to feed and all my stuff there."

"Is there a spare room?"

"Yes, but the bed isn't made up yet."

"I'll stop with you until this is resolved. I can bring my own bedding; we can pick it up on the way home. We'll take my car and I'll take a force radio. Is that okay with you, Saul?"

"Good idea, yes. You have my number if anything happens. I do need the bank book and details of the accounts."

"They're in my desk. I was going to sort it if I had time today. Before I found out about that. I'll get it for you. Will you come to the bank?"

"Yes. Now get home and can you please tell Diana everything. Thank you for your hard work today. Goodnight, ladies."

Diana and Jake met Julia and Sharon, as they drove into the farm. Diana invited them both in and asked them to bring her up to date on the events of the day. She explained that Saul had rung and updated her and suggested both of them might need to relax. The she said, "Don't worry, the dogs will see off anyone who tries to get in here. Incidentally, I thought you would like to know that we just shot down a drone that was flying over the farm, luckily before it got anywhere near the cottage. I told Saul and he is checking to see who it is registered to, if anyone, and we have disabled everything in and on it."

They had a wonderful meal and rather too much excellent wine before Sharon and Julia were walked down to the cottage and Jake checked everything before bidding them goodnight.

Chapter 7

Having arrived very early the next morning in the office, Saul made himself a strong coffee and briefed Alan, Geoff and Paul when they arrived an hour later. He joined Sharon, with Julia, at the bank, where they were ushered in to see the manager, a Mr Edwards. Sharon produced identification to him, and he said, "Well, you are definitely not the person who claimed to be you. I have the CCTV footage of when she came in and I have kept it to produce to you, Superintendent."

Sharon opened another account and froze the joint account, at the request of the bank. Saul ensured that her money was safe and had already made arrangements with headquarters for Sharon's wages to be paid into a new account. Then he handed a note to Julia and said, "Can you go and see this solicitor now, he's expecting you. I need to remain here for a bit. Meet back at the office when you're done."

When they had left Saul turned and asked the manager, "Tell me, Mr Edwards this £20,000, how was it paid in, cash, cheque banker's order?"

"Cash, all of it, in bundles of old notes. I wasn't happy about it at the time but the woman, who claimed to be Miss Wright, insisted it was from the sale of a car.

She even produced documentation for it, a vintage Rolls Royce, that she said her father had left her. I took copies just to be on the safe side, actually without her knowledge, and I have kept the money, sealed, as it came to us. I actually spoke to our fraud department about it yesterday. They said to notify the police, but you rang this morning before I could do so."

" I'll arrange to get it checked as soon as we can. I think it might be from a building society robbery about six weeks ago. If so, it's marked and was heading for destruction at the Bank of England."

"What do I do about Mr Gilchrist? I haven't seen him in quite a while. Should I inform him the account is frozen under an investigation?"

"He is the one under investigation."

"Oh, I thought he was a police officer."

"He was."

"Then I had better tell you, he has four other accounts here, two in his name and two with other partners. One is a man called Toller, the other a Mandy O'Dell. Do I freeze them too?"

"Yes, I'll get a court order for you to do so, as soon as I can. Gilchrist is now wanted for several offences."

"This is dreadful, we have slipped up, I trusted him. Several of his friends have quite substantial accounts here that I have been worried about. He came in once and was with one of your senior officers, a chap called Spedding. He rather pompously introduced himself as an assistant chief constable. Gilchrist transferred a huge amount to him about four months ago, about half a million if I remember. I didn't handle it, one of my deputy managers did, he is from another branch. You will get this High Court order and is it your fraud squad who will be dealing with this investigation?"

"Probably them or the robbery squad. I'll do that now."

Saul, having called the Chief and Wally, as well as the robbery squad, arrived at the courts with a robbery squad officer. They went to see a High Court judge to get the necessary orders, and some warrants. Leaving the courts, he then visited the police headquarters where he went to the chief's office to explain what he had discovered.

The chief read through the evidence and proceeded to say, "Neither you, nor I can deal with this. Apart from anything else, you have enough to be getting on with. I understand that today they have found a fifth body. I need you doing that, not this. I'll ring the Home Office to get another force to do an independent investigation, and I am sure they will want to suspend ACC Spedding from his attachment to them. Now to practicality, are you happy to keep WPC Wright on your squad and are you convinced she is an innocent party, not one of the gang?"

"Pretty convinced. I need to keep her safe and can best do that while she is working close to me."

"Yes. I'll tell everyone here who needs to know, and only them. How are you getting on with these murders?"

"We have two suspects and we believe the whole thing is connected to a paedophile ring. It's going to be a long drawn out job, but I'm working with the help of another agency. I am also working with the Lancashire force."

"Yes, I know that. You have worked with that agency before. You know I was warned about you before I took this post, that you have an uncanny knack of discovering things that are going wrong. I am just so thankful that my informant was right."

"Who was that informant?"

"That agency. Enough said."

Saul went into the squad office, caught up on what progress had been made and then went to the mortuary. Once again, he attended the post-mortems of the five bodies that had been discovered. They were all boys. Two of them had been provisionally identified from clothing and pictures. He then visited the forensic science laboratory where a large team were finding some helpful results. While he was there, he got a call from the computer department, which was in a nearby building, and went to see what they had found.

He went to the head investigator's office and was told, "These videos you seized from that caravan and some of the other stuff, we can connect directly with the Stevens boy, and the laptop from the caravan is connected to many other computers and devices. Then the CDs, those we have taken a brief look at, seem to be snuff movies. Before long, we will have some pictures of some of the people involved, but there are three women's voices on some of them. If you thought the Moors Murders tapes were bad, I warn you this is worse, much worse"

Saul spent the rest of the day collecting results, dishing out enquiries and just before the end of the working day he called into the office of the force psychiatrist.

"Saul, how can I help? I understand you are dealing with a massive case."

"Yes, Ashley I am, and I'm worried. It looks as though we are dealing with a massive paedophile ring and the murders of a number of boys, and at least one family, consisting of the parents and a boy and a little girl. I'm distressed by this, who wouldn't be, but as you know I have my own way of coping, used over many years. What I'm worried about is how it may affect the members of my squad. They're not all as hardened to it as I am. Nor do I want them trying to cope out of loyalty to me, or the squad. I need you to come and speak to everyone and tell them if they cannot cope or are finding it too hard, then they can work on something else for a while or leave the squad temporarily. I don't want to be responsible for the breakdown of any of my officers."

"I see. I wish more senior officers were as concerned about the mental welfare of their subordinates. Have you run it past the chief?"

"Yes, he agrees with me and wants you or one of your team to take it on. I want everyone on my team spoken to, individually, so they can opt out without being penalised in any way."

"Everyone?"

"Yes."

"Including you?"

"I can cope."

"Really? I will be at your squad office with a team first thing in the morning and you will also be part of this. If you are seen to be interviewed, it will make the others accept it easier. See you tomorrow."

Once again Saul was late home, having written up and signed off many documents, overtime sheets and other correspondence that came with being the one in charge. He drove home and once there Anna took one look at him and said, "Go to bed and get a proper night's sleep."

He did not even have the energy to argue with her and she brought him up a light meal and a drink. He was asleep within minutes of her going back downstairs.

The next morning when he went into work there was a rota where all officers were designated to an interview with the welfare department. Saul was not really surprised when he was hauled in first and answered a number of questions, and then told he could go back to his duties. He busied himself with organising a series of actions to be done that day and then went off to the timber yard to see how things were progressing. On the way he received a call from Diana which changed his destination and he returned to sort out an ongoing operation. He was worried about the apparent disappearance of Bill Birtwhistle. He had not been seen for twenty-four hours. He sent Alan and Tarik back to the woods at Elslack, to check if he had turned up at the caravan. When they rang a little later to say they had found Bill's body in the ditch, Saul's concern increased. The scenes of crime units were already working overtime and the whole case was getting too big. He had requested some help from neighbouring forces, which had been willingly given. On this occasion it seemed that the murder had occurred in Lancashire. He rang his opposite number there, whom he had worked with on several occasions.

"Hello, Keith, it's Saul Catchpole. You know what has happened? We found a body on your patch but it's connected with a case I am dealing with."

"Yes, Saul, I was just going to ring you, I think we need to combine. Shall I come to you or do I set up an incident room here?"

"We're up and running already. I'll find offices and accommodation for you."

"On my way then. Er, do I have to read up on animal traits?"

"It's got that far already? Oh hell! I'll tell you about it when you get here. I'm starting to see the funny side of it now, just."

He called in as many senior officers and sergeants as he could and said, "We need help. The score of bodies is now ten. Lancashire are coming to join us and other forces as well. Caroline, please will you deal with the next of kin and identifications. Can you also handle and liaise with the coroner's office for me? Use the families unit. The press release has gone out. One of the missing boys that we have found, or think we have, is Darren Cole, who has been missing eight months. Another one, we think over a year. We are setting up victim support and counselling. The WRVS have been wonderful and have even arranged to accommodate any next of kin. They've already supplemented us with catering wagons. The press office is giving four hourly updates. On a personal note, I want to say that we need to be at our fittest for this, so you must get a decent amount of sleep. Sergeant Bickerstaff is now acting inspector, and Julia is now an acting sergeant. Mr Dunlop is the office manager for here and we are getting in some more staff. DI Withers is now acting chief inspector and he wishes to allocate other tasks to you all. Those of you who have already been notified will be going with me for an operation this afternoon. It is Operation Primate. All of you on my squad, if you have not already been spoken to by the welfare department, will be seen today. I will tell you why. The kind of offences we're dealing with are horrific and can have a traumatic effect on us. They are distressing and anyone, and I mean anyone, who does not wish to deal with this will be allowed to move to other duties for the duration of this case, without any slur on your record. Yes, I have already been counselled and you can ask for help at any time. I do not want anyone staying on the unit to deal with things that distress them just out of loyalty either to me, the job or the unit."

"Sir, why primate?"

"No, Peter, it is not related to my apparently amusing outburst about animal behaviour the other day, it is because the people in this target group have a fear of monkeys."

"Travellers, you mean."

"Correct. I want you to also have rest days. You're not expected to work all your days off. If any of you choose to volunteer to work, one day extra a week, you will be recompensed accordingly. Now, another thing I wish to make quite clear, is that in my experience the travelling community, well, Romany folk at least, have a very strict set of moral rules. Okay, they don't quite match ours, but the kind of thing we are investigating is something they will not tolerate. I have made some enquiries about this particular group that we are looking at, and they are shunned by many other travellers. That tells me they're doing something very wrong indeed.

Now sort yourselves out and find what duties you have today, please. Sharon, Geoff, Alan, Paul and Julia, a quick word."

Chapter 8

Petunia, normally a bit weird, was displaying some odd behaviour, even for her. She wandered round the camp, unable to concentrate on anything. Even smoking a spliff did not seem to help. No matter what she tried, she couldn't get her worries to go away. One thing that did not worry her was Reuben's absence as he would have asked her awkward questions.

Petunia was very, very, frightened. She knew far too much and the others in the camp knew it. She had realised why they had insisted on her fetching the firewood. They had meant her to find the body, she knew that. It was a warning to her to keep her mouth shut. Her wanderings at odd times had meant that she had seen and heard things that maybe she should not have heard. Whilst she had little to do with children, she knew that harming them was wrong, dreadfully wrong. Then someone had seen her watching one day. They had been on their way to the Appleby Horse Fair and had gone to *that* timber yard. Caleb and his family had gone for the wood on that occasion. She had wandered off while she was waiting for some of the firewood to be put in her van and had come across something odd. They had, she later discovered, missed her. Then, at Appleby, she had been offered some free drugs by Caleb. She knew then that something was amiss. She had not used them and had reluctantly thrown them away. Then there was an accident that she had narrowly avoided. They had been changing a wheel on her van. She knew the jack they were using was not hers or Reuben's. She wisely put some rocks under the axel when the wheel was taken off, and when the jack collapsed, she was not crushed, as would have been the case if she had not put the stones there as a precaution. Since then she had felt more and more like an outsider. Reuben had not even listened to her fears. He was very insensitive anyway. She knew she should tell someone but could not trust anyone. If she ran away, they would find her. She made a point of keeping everything of value to her on her person, so she could get away if the opportunity arose.

She saw the horse dealer chap and his woman arrive in the camp. He wasn't a real vet, just a bloke with a way with horses. He was a big chap with red hair and blue eyes. She almost considered him a Viking. His woman was very ordinary, quiet, and said very little. Petunia watched as the woman fetched some things from the Land Rover that they had come in.

She remembered that this woman and her bloke had been at Appleby and had helped at a foaling. She watched as they walked across the camp site. Usually dogs would rush up to and growl at any uninvited stranger, but this time all the dogs rushed up, wagged their tails and sat quietly by the woman. This struck Petunia as very strange and she looked, properly, for the first time at the woman. The woman looked up at Petunia and their eyes met. There was something comforting in her direct gaze, something trustworthy. Petunia went to her caravan and made a pot of tea. She thought for a few minutes and with a mug of tea came out again and offered it to the woman who was waiting while the red headed man was cold shoeing a horse. The woman walked back to the van with her, having accepted the mug of tea, and sat down on the van steps beside her. They sat in silence for a while, and then the woman said, "You are troubled, frightened."

"I am, yes."

"Go to the coppers, tell them."

"I can't."

"They can help you; they are the only ones who can."

"If I do, I'm as good as dead."

"If you don't, they will get you anyway. You choose."

"How can I get away without being seen?"

"Come with us, ask us for a lift into town."

"I can't."

"We'll be back soon, thanks for the tea".

A little later, Petunia was sitting by her van, when one of the men in the group came up to her and asked, "What did you say to her?"

"Who?"

"The horse doctor's woman."

"Nothing much. She thanked me for the tea, and said it was a nice day."

"Well, don't talk to anyone, not even them."

"I won't."

She felt a shiver go down her spine. She was being watched and he was telling her so. She went back into her caravan, wishing Rueben was there.

In the magistrate's court Reuben pleaded guilty to theft, paid his fine and £20 costs, before being released. He headed out of town as fast as he could by hitching a lift. He was totally unaware that he was being followed. He arrived at the camp and went to his caravan. He noticed Petunia seemed quite with it, for her.

"I didn't expect you back out for a while."

"I got a fine, stupid magistrates couldn't make up their minds what to do with me. I expected a spell in stir, so I paid up and got out of there. Anything new?"

"No. I'm glad to see you, I've missed you. I'll get us something to eat."

Reuben was pleasantly surprised. During the afternoon Petunia was most attentive, hardly moving more than ten metres from him. He was not the most sensitive of men and it took some time for him to realize there was something wrong. Once back in their van he asked, "Is everything all right?"

"Not really, no. I think I want to break off from this group. Can we go somewhere on our own for a bit?"

"S'pose so, it might be a good idea. Wait until we break camp, we'll fall behind and then go over to Liverpool, and get a ferry over to Ireland. I think we have enough cash."

"I've got some too."

Reuben wondered who she had fallen out with, but he was happy to travel alone for a while. He never liked to hang around an area where the police knew him.

The camp was due to break up that evening and everyone was packing up. They set fire to some of the rubbish they had left behind and got the mare and her foal into a horse box for travelling. As they drove out of the site, Reuben and Petunia waited and tagged onto the back of the convoy. A few miles down the road there was a bit of a hold up, so they waited until they could turn off on another road. Then they saw why there was a hold up, there were police everywhere. Some officers advanced towards Reuben's van and he began to protest when he was asked to get out. Then it dawned on him it was not him they wanted; it was Petunia. He wondered why. In amongst some of the officers documenting the raid was the plain clothed policeman who had arrested him. The man spoke, addressing Petunia,

"Mary Alison Letts, I am arresting you for theft."
He then cautioned her.

"Her name is Petunia; you got the wrong one!"

"I know it is, but no, we have not. Now, I have here a warrant to search this caravan and vehicle. All the

131

vans are being searched. You will remain here while it is done, except her. Take her away please, Officer."

Petunia did not protest; she meekly went off with the two policewomen. Reuben thought she looked rather relieved. He began to have a very bad feeling about it. He normally paid little attention to what the others did in the camp and wondered what had warranted such a massive police operation. They were looking very hard for something. When they got to Caleb's very large caravan, they arrested Caleb and his two brothers Cain and Aaron, and their vans were seized as well. Caleb's wife, Mabel, was most vociferous and called the plain clothes policeman every unsavoury thing she could think of.

Rueben heard a uniformed office say to her, "Colourful, but believe me, you are not even in the same league as him." Nodding towards Saul he added, "If you carry on, he'll nick you too. Then we'll have to take your kids into care."

Mabel shut up, very quickly.

Left without their leader, the group decided to stay put on the wide grass verges of the country road they were on for the night. They unpacked what they needed and when the police had finally gone, Mabel said, "They nicked him for murder. He ain't no murderer. What they nick Petunia for?"

"Theft. Where are you and the kids going to sleep?"

"I'll move in with Seth. What has Petunia been nicking then?"

"The only thing I can think of is the wood."

"Oh, yes. Oh, I think I'll give our solicitor chap a ring. The bastards took me phone, anyone got one?"

Reuben handed her his phone and went back to his van.

Petunia was taken to a cell block in a large police station where she was searched, booked in, and given her rights. She asked, "What is it you think I stole?"

The reply was, "Firewood from a wood yard."

"That. I don't want a solicitor but I ain't saying anything until I see the person in charge, about them bodies you've been finding"

"What do you know, then?"

"I ain't telling you, I want to talk to the big boss."

"You're in luck then, that is who is going to talk to you anyway. Chief Superintendent Catchpole."

"Well, I ain't saying nothing to no one else."

"Fine, wait in the cell. He won't be long. I'll get you something to eat."

Caleb, who had been taken to another police station, had a very bad feeling. One of scared apprehension. Bill had already told him the police were suspicious and had been sniffing around a bit too much. He had taken action about Bill; the man had been useful in the past, but his usefulness was over. Bill had never felt the blow to the head that had killed him, and they had covered his body with undergrowth not far from his caravan. Caleb hoped Aaron and Cain knew better than to talk, but he was afraid that Cain might let the cat out of the bag as he was easily intimidated. He asked to see Cain and was told he was at another station and no, he was not permitted to see anyone, and the only call he could make was to a solicitor.

Alan Withers came into the cell block a few moments later and said,

"You are under arrest for the suspected murder of an Arnold Stevens, a Jason Stevens and a Bettina Stevens. You do not have to say anything unless you wish to do so, but it may harm your defence if you do not mention when questioned, something that you later rely on in court. All this will be explained in due course, but first we need to take some samples, DNA, and fingerprints. We will also need to take some clothes from you, so there is clothing you can change into in your cell."

"What if I don't cooperate?

"The samples will be taken by force, if necessary"

"All right then."

By the time they were booked in, fed and samples taken, it was deemed necessary for them all to have a rest period. They were bedded down in the cells for the night, and told to expect interviews in the morning which surprisingly, all those detained, agreed to.

Chapter 9

Saul was already in the office when Alan arrived, who looked at him and said,

"Saul, you look exhausted. How much sleep have you had over the last week? You are insisting we get enough rest; it surely applies to you as well."

"Not a lot. It goes with the job, I can survive on cat naps for a while and if you don't take that supercilious grin off your face, I'll cry."

"Sorry, I forgot, no animal cracks."

"Correct. I'll collect Sharon, and interview Petunia, and you and Paul please deal with Caleb, Cain and Aaron. Oh well done, Paul, you are early. Are you able to go with Alan here?"

"Yes, eager and willing, sir. I will be most interested to hear their explanation."

As Sharon and Saul walked down to the car, Sharon said, "Sir, why me? You must have more experienced officers?"

"DI Withers suggested it would be very good experience for you and that you have a calming presence. Now, have you had any more problems with Tony or his mates?"

"None, sir. Julia stayed, but has now gone home."

They ushered Petunia into an interview room and after the usual formalities and explanations she was offered a solicitor although she declined one, saying, "What I have to say is to you, and no one else. Are you the man in charge?"

"I am, yes, and this officer is here as we need a woman present."

"I want to do a deal with you."

"I don't do deals. You have been cautioned and given your rights. Now let me tell you, I know you were at the timber yard and that you took wood from there using their trolley. Your DNA was found by the wood pile where the bodies were discovered. That I can prove."

"You can actually prove that?"

"I can. Now tell me what you know, or I will get on, charge you, and release you. I think all you did was find the body and steal some firewood."

"No, don't release me, please. All right I will tell you, but if I do, I want protection, and the charges against me dropped and a new identity."

"I will promise nothing. Let's hear what you have to say first. Then I will consider what to do."

"I found the body, well, all I found was a hand sticking out of a black bin bag. I jumped back and fell over and grazed my knee."

"And left threads of fabric there, and on the hole in the fence, and some blood on the trolley. We traced the DNA from the blood and came up with you."

"All right! I admit all that. Now if I tell you the rest, you must look after me. My finding it was no accident. I was meant to. It was a message to me to keep my mouth shut."

"Go on."

"I've been with this group of travellers for about three years, since I met up with Reuben. He's been with them about five. I don't have much to do with the others, they think I am strange and rather ignore me, because I go walkabout in my head sometimes."

"Are you on anything now?"

"No, I needed to have my wits about me. I think they were trying to kill me because of what I might have seen or know. That was while Reuben was inside, I was more at risk then."

"Who are they?"

"Caleb, Aaron, Cain, Seth and their cronies. We travel all over you see. I think that's why I liked being with the group. Often Caleb would go off, meet people, locally, I mean. Sometimes Cain and Aaron went too. I went into town once and saw Caleb with a kid, a boy about ten, I reckon. It was at a park. I didn't think anything off it, not then. We moved on from there."

"Would you recognise this boy?"

"Might do, it were about a year ago, it was in Cheshire, just outside the Wirral. Anyway, Caleb never lets anyone, bar his own family, inside his caravan, ever. This boy wore a bright turquoise tee shirt. I remembered it because I thought it was a good colour for a bit of art

I was doing. It had like a smiley face on the back, an emoji thing. We came back to outside Leeds again. Two weeks later Caleb's nephew was wearing it. Another kid in the group had this boy's baseball cap, also bright blue. They said Caleb had said they could have them after Mabel had washed them. I don't have a telly, well not really, but I heard a kid had gone missing from there. Never connected it till later. Then we went down to Shropshire. I went into Ludlow to get stuff and we was parked up at a place called Brimfield Cross. In Ludlow I saw Caleb and Aaron talking to another boy, about twelve he were.

"He was wearing a Black Sabbath tee shirt. Caleb clocked me and later told me the boy had asked to come and see the horses. Funny, because the horses were at the camp, not in the town. We came back to this area soon afterwards, I got a bit nosy and looked in Caleb's van when he was not there, through the window, like. I saw the tee shirt."

"The one the boy had been wearing, how did you know it was the same one?"

"It had a jagged tear on the left sleeve. We went down to Devon and Wiltshire and Somerset, then to Glastonbury. I got into the festival, even sold some pictures and a bit of art there but got caught, and as I hadn't got a ticket, got thrown out. I walked into the town and went up to the Tor, very fine that is, and then I went down to the chapel remains at the bottom of a hill. Some old church, I think. Caleb was there, again with two young boys. I pretended I hadn't seen him. They looked like twins. Both blonde, really pale hair. I went and got some sculpture from my van, went back into town and some arty shop gave me good money for them. Then Caleb disappeared for three days, left his van locked and went off in his transit. When he drove off in it, he had those two boys with him. But when he came back three days later, he didn't."

"Where did you go after that?"

"New Forest, then over to Sussex, Surrey and up through Bedfordshire. Caleb would go off from time to time then come back. I didn't think no more, not really, until we came up and camped on our way to Appleby. We came to the same woodyard for some firewood then. It was evening and I was waiting with some of the others in the auction mart car park with my van, waiting to go and get the wood. That time the gate had been conveniently left open for us. I was a bit surprised when we left that Mabel locked it up again, with her own key. Anyway, while we were waiting, I wanted a wee so I wandered off into some scrubland. I had my wee and as I was about to go back, I heard some voices. I was well hidden in the bushes. There was this family, the bloke looked most respectable, and a tiny woman, he had a toddler in a pushchair. There was a boy talking to Caleb. The man said something like, 'Do you really think we would let him meet a complete stranger off the net on his own? Of course we came, and we don't like what we have found. Arnold, come here, this man is no friend.

He is one of those men we told you about. Betty, call the police, back to the car now!' Then Aaron appeared and handed Caleb something metal. It looked like a gun. I didn't want to see any more, so I went into the bushes, and back round another way to wait by the van. I saw Cain driving a strange car later and Caleb told me if I said anything about what they were doing I would have a nasty accident."

"Did you hear any shots?"

"Didn't expect to. Caleb has a silencer on his gun but no, I didn't. When I found the body a couple of weeks later, I saw the man from the yard cutting the hole in the fence for me to get in. The older one what is seeing the woman from the yard."

"Did Caleb say anything more?"

"Not directly, no, but he kept looking at me. It was him gave me some free smack at Appleby, but it didn't look right so I threw it away. Then there was his jack that collapsed when we was changing a wheel on my van. Luckily, I had put a load of stones under the axle so it didn't come down on me when the jack folded. It was him insisted I went and got the wood from the yard the other day. He made a big thing of it. He knew what I would find, I'm sure. It was at least a warning."

"Has he said anything else?"

"Only wanting to know what the horse doctor's woman said to me or more accurately, what I had said to her. I gave her a cup of tea. She told me to go to you. Even gave me a number to ring, I never did. It was scratched on a thin wafer biscuit, so I ate it, rather than Caleb finding it. She knew I was worried."

"Was she in on this?"

"No way. They come sometimes, just to help with the horses. He is a giant of a man, same coloured hair as you, but much longer. Blue eyes too. Actually, he looks a bit like you. He bought a foal from us last year. I never really noticed her before, she don't push herself forward, although I did notice that she has an amazing way with dogs; they absolutely adore her. Ruben and I was going to break off just before you stopped us. I was trying not to think about it. I'll be honest with you; I've been fuddled on drugs for months. I was going to ring that number as soon as we got to Liverpool. If they find me, I'll be dead. It's only since I came off the drugs a bit, that I realized what I saw and heard."

Sharon asked, "Before you became a traveller, what did you do?"

"Believe it or not I was a teacher, an art teacher. Then I got into drugs, mainly through a boyfriend and left my previous life behind. I bummed around, got into trouble and then met Reuben. Sad, I know."

Saul said, "Can you remember any dates?"

"I don't know what month it is most of the time, let alone what day. I remember seasons. Are you going to help me?"

"That rather depends on your agreeing to give evidence, I know you don't want to, you're frightened, but if you do I can get you on a drug rehabilitation course where you'll be safe, and then once you've given evidence, a new identity, under the Witness Protection programme. You will only get that if you stay on the course, get free of drugs and give evidence. Why do you call yourself Petunia?"

"It was a nickname to start with, I used to smoke a lot of pot, and used petunia oil to hide the smell. As you say, my real name is Mary. What about the theft?"

"I think Petunia could get a verbal warning."

"I won't be Petunia no more, will I?"

"No. Give this some thought, it means splitting with Reuben, never seeing him or anyone else from the camp again."

"Where will I be going?"

"Is there anywhere that no one knows you?"

"I'm originally from the Black Country, never been to Kent mind, nor Norfolk or Suffolk."

She turned to Sharon and said, "Can I trust him? Will he do all that for me?"

"Yes, I trust him, have done with my life. I don't think you'll get a better deal."

"Okay, you've got a deal. It's about time I went back to being proper anyway."

Saul and Sharon left that station and drove to the murder squad office. On the journey, Saul asked, "What did you make of that?"

"It had the ring of truth and explains a lot. I am wondering if some of it was her imagination."

"'I'm not sure any of it was. She told us several things I didn't know. Like the woman seeing Bill."

"Yes, but I think I already knew that woman at the yard wasn't right."

"How old would you say Mrs Moreby is, have you met her?"

"Yes. I saw her at the yard when we were digging. I thought she was his wife, not the mother of the foreman. I'd put her at the most, forty-five, fifty at a stretch. She dresses older."

"Women are much better at judging the age of other women. How old do you think Moreby is?"

"About forty, forty-two?"

"I got Nita to do some digging. She's his stepmother. The local beat bobby got chatting to some of the inmates at the old folk's home in the village. Very revealing indeed. Apparently, there was quite a scandal about it at the time. She was old Mr. Moreby's secretary. The old man was arrested for interfering with children and she was suspected of procuring them for him. But he topped himself in prison before it got to court and the charges were dropped. All years ago."

"Funny, she thought you looked like Jake, and this woman has a way with dogs. "

"Keep those thoughts to yourself, you're brighter than I thought, Diana certainly thinks so."

At another station, Alan and Paul were interviewing Caleb. To almost every question his reply was, "No comment." He refused to even give a proper identity. The only thing he said was that he wished to speak to his nephews, Aaron, Cain and Seth, and was visibly angry when he was told he couldn't. His solicitor had been contacted and, on hearing the allegations, told the officers that he no longer wished to represent any of the family. The interview was adjourned until another solicitor could be found. They then began interviewing Aaron, who talked for a long time after a solicitor had attended and spoken to him. The solicitor had prepared a long and detailed statement, which he gave to Aaron and then read it for him as Aaron openly admitted he could not read or write. Aaron clarified several matters and then put his mark on the statement. As the interview ended Aaron said, "To be honest I am glad it is over. I know I'm due a long time in prison, but compared to what I and Cain have been putting up with for the last ten years or so, it will be heaven. You have no idea how vile Caleb is. Mabel isn't much better."

Cain needed no encouragement to talk. He did not want a solicitor at all and asked for no deals. He explained his part in many horrors. He then said, "I only did it to stop him getting to my kids. He said he'd leave them alone if I helped him get other kids. He's been using me since I was seven. He stopped fancying me when I got to fourteen. He did it to Aaron too and I think Seth. He and Bill, they've known each other for many years. I know they sold a lot of the films they made to rich men that they knew. I'll even tell you where he keeps the films and pictures."

"Where?"

"Him and Bill had run it out of the timber yard, with Bill's woman. She helped Caleb to get the kids. In her house is a cellar, hidden behind a pantry door. We had to take boxes of films and stuff there. Caleb and Bill paid her for it. That's all she likes, is money. She hid it because she couldn't trust that stepson of hers. She hates him 'cos he was left the yard by his dad, who were a wrong'un too. She wanted it."

"Are you prepared to make a statement and give evidence about all this in court?"

"Can't read or write well, but yes, I will. Caleb made sure we never got to do much schooling in case we told someone. I must not go to the same prison as him, though. You see, I can never remember not being scared of him. I will admit what I have done and once he's inside my kids and my woman will be free. I think Aaron might as well. If Aaron wants to see me, I'll talk to him. My woman can go back to the proper Romany family if I'm not with her."

"Where were your parents?"

"Good question. They just suddenly disappeared, and we never saw or heard from them again. Caleb said they had gone back to Romania. They left all their money and all their things and just went one night. I wonder if he didn't knock them off to get us boys. He made out he and Mabel were being so kind, taking us in. I think you will find he's got rid of Bill too."

"I will talk to the CPS about this and come back to you."

By lunch time they were back at the office and Saul sat down with all the detectives on the team and told them what had been divulged. Saul then went off to obtain several warrants, leaving Paul and Geoff to interview Caleb, who had by this time found a solicitor. It was not a successful interview and Caleb began behaving very oddly. He started to say he was hearing voices and he was the tool of Satan, and nothing was his fault. The solicitor looked as surprised as did both the officers, and after the rather short interview, Caleb was charged with the murder of Arnold Stevens and Bettina Stevens and then returned to his cell.

Saul rushed to the office and gathered a team and they set off, arriving at Elizabeth Moreby's house. She invited them into her lounge and graciously offered them a cup of tea, and Saul politely declined and then she said, "I expect you have come to tell me how things are progressing?"

"In a way, yes. I have some bad news. Bill's body was found yesterday up near his caravan in the woods. He had been murdered."

"Oh, that's terrible, so sad. I didn't know him that well, but he worked for us for ten years. How awful!"

"Yes, isn't it? Did he ever come here?"

"Occasionally. I knew he had a caravan somewhere; we were not that close."

"So you never had a relationship with him?"

"What a suggestion! Actually, I thought he was gay."

"Did you know he was a paedophile?"

"No, how dreadful! I don't approve of the kind of thing! If I'd known I would have got Bob to sack him."

"Did he or any of his friends ever leave anything here?"

"No, never. I don't think he had any friends."

"So you don't mind if we search the house?"

"Yes, I do mind. You would have to have a warrant."

"We have one, here. Here is your copy. Shall we start in the kitchen?"

"You can't do this; I'm a respectable woman. This is my house and I want you out, now!"

"Yes, Mrs Moreby, we can, and I know that this house is owned by your stepson, not you. He is at one of our police stations at the moment and has, in fact given us permission, but tells us that he has not been able to access parts of the house for some years and that you have the keys to the cellar and the loft access. He also tells us that you are far from respectable. We also know you are involved in several unlawful acts, you see, the others have talked."

Elizabeth Moreby changed into a hissing venomous virago. Gone was the respectability. She flew at Saul, nails out, and tried to scratch his face. She was not a tall woman and could not reach, and within seconds she was held and cuffed by Sharon and a uniform WPC.

"Elizabeth Moreby, I am arresting you for conspiracy to murder and aiding and abetting obscene publication. Are you going to tell us where the keys are, or do we have to break the doors down?"

"Go to hell!"

She was placed into the back of a police van and searched. Minutes later, Sharon returned with a set of keys that had been found on a chain around the woman's waist.

"It's okay, sir, we videoed how we found them, they were on chain which was woven into a plaited leather belt. She is screaming that no one will believe that we found them on her and that we must have planted them. She does not know yet, that there was a video running. So far, she has kicked two officers and spat at all of us."

"Is anyone hurt?"

"Not badly. She has totally lost it. If she's respectable, then I'm the Queen of Sheba. They're taking her straight to custody. I have cautioned her, several times, but every time I try to say anything, she screams foul abuse at me. It's all on tape. No wonder the stepson is so scared of her. We also found a taser in her handbag. Cain said we would, didn't he?"

"Indeed, he did. Now let's find this cellar."

The cellar was large, well-lit, with a camera and screen set up, and seats placed for a show. There were hundreds of tapes, films and CDs, DVDs on shelves, in boxes some of which were addressed and looked ready for posting; their contents were declared as educational videos. In the loft they found several trunks full of tapes and a number of photographs, mainly, but not exclusively, of young boys and of men abusing them. The vans in which they were secured to be taken back and examined were being driven off, when Saul came across one uniformed officer, a young PC, sitting on the verge of the lane, who looked rather unwell. As Saul approached the officer was violently sick, "I'm sorry, sir, I shouldn't have chucked up. It's just I saw some of those photos and it makes me cringe. I know, I'm a wuss."

"No, you're not. You are sensitive and there's nothing wrong with that. There's nothing wrong with being distressed by horrific things like this. Sergeant, please take this officer back to his station, sit him down, give him some tea or coffee and put him on other duties. This will not go against him at all, he is to be commended for being so concerned."

"I agree, sir. I feel pretty sick at what we found. It is all right, lad, you're not alone; at least you had the guts to admit how you feel. It's the ones who hide their feelings we have to watch out for."

Back at the office Saul briefed everyone: "Some of you may be aware that there is more than one case running at the moment and both are very big. The Home Office have appointed a DCC Owen, from Northumberland Constabulary, to take over one of these cases, which may involve some officers from this force to be investigated. The other case, that of the murders, is getting huge. We have drafted in as many officers as we can find, so I want you to split up and each have an officer that has been drafted in to assist you. Because of this we have to be squeaky clean and prepared to have everything inspected and assessed. In other words, we do it utterly by the book. Tidy your desks and get ready. Don't let me down."

He went to check the mail on his desk. One was a message to ring Diana, which he promptly did.

"Diana, it's Saul. What's happened.?"

"Gilchrist or his mates have been here. Nick and John chased them off. Jake and I were out. I left a package for you; did you get it?"

Saul looked on his desk and after moving the huge pile of papers and statements he found it. "Yes, it's here."

"It's self-explanatory. Oh and Petunia is ready to talk."

"Yes, we nicked her and she's telling us lots."

"Get Sharon to come to us first. Tell her Mung is fine. I need to tell you much more soon. Come when you can."

Saul called Sharon into his office a little while later.

"Your pendant, Sharon. I'll tell you now, inside it was a chip, it has been deactivated and removed. That's how they knew where you were. Do you want it back?"

"No, thanks, I've remembered a couple of months ago, when we had a row, Tony broke it or said it was broken. He took it, and got it repaired. He was full of apologies and I thought he meant it."

"Have you seen the new investigating officer?"

"Yes, Mr Owen, I saw him this morning he said you had asked for me to stay on your team, that I was needed. Thank you."

"It wasn't just for your sake; I can assure you. I need you, will do for some time. Things are happening. I have just rung Mr Owen and told him. Diana and Jake had visitors today, so she wants you to go straight to her for a meal. Mung is fine. I want you to do exactly what she says as if she were my rank or higher."

"I understand, she is anyway, I think. Something like MI5."

"She said you were bright. If your diary is complete, and everything marked up, I want you to go home now."

When Sharon had gone Saul called Julia in. "Julia, will you please talk to Mabel Jones, tomorrow. She may be very difficult but may know a lot. Can you take one of the Lancashire lasses with you, a WDC Cox, who has a good liaison with travellers."

"Yes, I know her, we were at training school together. Are you going home soon?"

"I'm afraid I'm going to have to. If I don't get some sleep, I'll drop off my perch. My mind is scrambled as it is. Stop grinning!"

"No comment, goodnight, sir."

Saul made it home at a reasonable hour and even managed a refreshing walk with his two dogs, before sitting down in his armchair. His wife woke him about eleven and sent him up to bed.

Chapter 10

Sharon knocked at the farmhouse door and heard Diana shout, "Come in Sharon, mind the puppy!"

Once in, Sharon was greeted by the dogs and a new addition, another dog, "Mr Catchpole said I needed to see you. Isn't this puppy wonderful! I didn't know you were getting another."

"I need to explain. Meet Janet, a friend of ours. She farms not far from here. It's actually her puppy. Sit down do, tea is in teapot. That pup is sister to my white faced one, and the other one. I wondered if you wanted it. Janet says it isn't up to sheep work, it's a bit too soft, but will make a loving and good pet. It can run with mine whenever you're not here. It already knows about cats. Are you interested?"

"What's her name?"

Janet said, "She is registered as Flyte, but I've always called her Boo."

"How much do you want for her?"

"Just a good loving home. I sold the rest of the litter, so I've more than covered my costs. She is registered, inoculated, chipped and insured, if you want to take her on. I brought all the documentation with me, together with some food, a couple of spare bowls, collar and lead, and a dog bed that I don't use any more, just to get you started."

"I would love to, Boo, here girl." Boo snuggled up to Sharon who immediately fell in love with her. Janet smiled and said, "I hoped she would find a loving home; it looks like she has, I must be getting back, I'm already full of food. I can barely walk! Sharon, you are welcome to come and visit me, and if you ever need a bolt hole, come to me. See you soon."

Janet patted Boo on the head and then left.

Sharon looked at Diana saying, "You organized that. Thank you. I think she's just what I need, at the moment. Will you help me train her? I think I owe you."

"No, actually you don't. I'm just pleased she has a home. I don't think it will be bad for you to have a dog to love and to protect you. Now, you need to know we had visitors, but Jake and I were out."

"Horse doctoring?"

"Yes, if you must know. I'd be grateful if you didn't tell anyone else that. Have you handed your bank books over to the investigating officer?"

"Yes."

"He came to see me this afternoon, when we got back. I told him all I could. The whole thing is getting rather sinister. I think there is still something they are after, that you have. You may not even know you have it. It may not just be the pendant."

"What? I only took what was mine."

"Would you mind if I searched your things?"

"No, not at all, although I did have a good look."

"I expect you have been very thorough. Maybe my search might find something, you know fresh eyes."

"May I be there?"

"Of course,"

"I might learn something. I know you are very senior at what it is you do."

"Fairly, yes. When this is over, I want to talk to you about that."

"Me? You think I could do what you do?"

"Possibly, we can discuss it in a year or so. Now, that is Jake coming in and supper is on the table."

The meal was, as usual, utterly delicious. Afterwards Sharon drove down to the cottage and Diana joined her with Boo, and they went inside. Boo's meeting with Mung went very well, Boo instantly accepting that Mung was the superior being. Diana briefly looked around and then took from her pocket a multi tooled penknife. She began in the kitchen and took apart every utensil she could, checking any place or cavity within them, then carefully put them back together again and checked that they worked.

"Tell you what, why don't you put the kettle on, this may take a while."

"That kettle doesn't work, the on switch is sticking."

"Just try it, I think it will now."

Sharon filled the kettle and switched it on and stood back in amazement when it worked. She had only kept the kettle for sentimental reasons and was planning to get it repaired.

"That was my parents' gift to me. Thank you."

They moved into the sitting room and Sharon watched. She had been taught how to search and thought she was rather good at it, but Diana was in a different league. She looked at and in everything that had come with Sharon's things. She took down the painting that Sharon had brought with her, looked at it, checked it, and said, "It's rather good. Pen-y-ghent, I think. Where did you get it?"

"I bought it at a sale for police charities last year, at the force open day."

"Yes, I thought so. Do you know who the artist is?"

"I can't make it out, all I can see are the initials, SMC"

"They stand for Saul Moses Catchpole, my brother-in-law. He is a very good artist, when he has the time. It is how he relaxes."

"I had no idea. He doesn't do animals, does he?"

They both laughed.

"Not at the moment I don't think."

The bathroom produced nothing, nor did the spare bedroom. In the main bedroom Diana checked a bedside lamp, a cuddly toy, and then picked up a photo in a frame from the bedside table.

She looked at it and said, "Who is this?"

"That was my mother. She died a few years ago, just after I left training school."

"It's a good photo, it must be very precious to you?"

"It is. I take it everywhere with me. Tony had it framed for me when we first got together. He was very nice then."

Diana felt the frame and said, "Its balance is out." She went over and sat on the bed and looked at the frame under the light of the bedside lamp. She turned it over and ran her fingers down the back edges of the frame. She fiddled briefly, then moved a small piece of the frame out and out tipped a key. She said, "Don't touch it. Get me an evidence bag from my jacket pocket."

Sharon did that. Once the key was safely bagged up, Diana said, "Had you any idea it was there?"

"None. I'm rather shocked."

"I bagged it so that we cannot find your fingerprints or DNA on it. So Tony cannot say you put it there. I expect we will find his. It looks like a safe deposit key. Did he handle the picture much?"

"Not that I ever saw, no."

"Was it ever moved?"

"I thought he had been dusting; but thinking about it, that never happened, that I saw. That was my job, so he said."

"Hmm. I'll just check the rest."

"You think there is more?"

"There might be. What else were you especially fond of, that you would never throw away?"

"My mother's locket in my jewellery pouch, in the top drawer of the chest of drawers there, and my photo album, on the bookcase. I unpacked the books yesterday."

Sharon went to the drawer and took out her locket and handed it to Diana saying, "I was wearing this yesterday."

"What is inside it?"

"A lock of my mother's hair."

"I need to look at it, do you mind?"

"Not at all, I haven't opened it in a long time."

Diana gently opened the locket. Sharon noticed she had on scenes of crime gloves. Gently, Diana probed the hair inside with a pair of tweezers. She removed a computer chip from under the hair and bagged it.

"Interesting. That's a tracer chip. So they could find your location or where you were living."

"The bastard!"

"I know. Let me check all the books and then I'll look at the album. Do you know how to properly check books?"

" I don't think I do, not the way you will. Please show me."

Sharon learned a lot in the next hour, about how to search. The books were checked in three ways, the spine was examined, the covers were felt and the pages checked individually. Then they turned to the photo album. Between two cleverly joined pages, behind a photo of Sharon's father, they found another key which was bagged. Diana then checked Sharon's bag, her purse and even her wristwatch.

Then they both sat in the sitting room and Sharon produced some gin and tonic, and they relaxed for a bit. She had put the dog bed in the corner of the sitting room with an old blanket.

"Listen, Sharon," Diana said, "I think we might have to set a trap. I'll have two identical keys made up and replace them. I will get copies of the photos as well. We need them to get in here to spring the trap. I'll put a hidden video surveillance camera in the sitting room and your bedroom, and outside to cover your car. Switch it on whenever you leave; er, did you want those old slippers?"

"What, oh no! Boo, no, not those please, Not allowed!"

Boo was happy with the old blanket, and went and laid on her bed, having had a cuddle with Sharon, and a telling off from Diana. Sharon fed her in the kitchen and made sure there was water in a bowl, and she also fed Mung, on an upper cupboard top.

They sat down again. Sharon asked, "What the hell is this all about do you think?"

"I'm pretty certain it is about a large amount of money and trying to shift the blame if they ever got caught out. You were to be the patsy. The safe deposit may even be in your name. Now they know the hunt is on, they will want to get the money and run, leaving you to face the music. Thank God Saul cottoned on when he did."

"I owe him, I know that. Did you know, he's starting to make jokes about animals now. It's very funny."

"I am ringing Mr Owen now. Boo, for all her bad ways will alert you to any strangers. She has already met Nick and John. If you're scared, go to either of them if we're not here. Here is an alarm that will alert me and Jake, and the two farm workers, that you're in trouble. Don't hesitate. Is there any more of that delicious gin?"

"Yes, here. Did I say, I actually discovered one of the bodies?"

"Well done, but not very pleasant, I expect?"

"It was exciting though."

"Yes, I know."

"From experience I suspect."

"True, did you want Boo chewing the rug? Try the old towel from the kitchen. Put it so she can steal it. Preferably with some food remains on it."

"I don't believe it; she's snuggling up to Mung!"

They had a pleasant chat, and later Sharon slept well, with Mung and Boo happily entwined at the foot of the bed.

The next morning Saul and Paul interviewed Caleb. They had to wait until the new solicitor had spoken with him, which had taken some time. At the interview, Caleb's attitude had changed. He happily, it seemed, admitted kidnapping and killing twelve boys and the Stevens family, with Bill. When asked about Bill, he admitted killing him as well. Then he went off on a rant about how he had to obey voices and was ordered by Satan, and it was not his fault. He explained in some detail how the voices would tell him when and what to do. They also told him that to complete his mission, he needed to drive a stake through the hearts of all of them. He told them that he had to direct his disciples, his nephews, Aaron, Cain and Seth, to do their master's bidding and that his wife, Mabel, was the one telling him, she was the voice of Satan.

Saul let him rant for a while before saying, "I wonder if you can help me. I am making enquiries into the disappearance of Ruth and Mark Jones, your brother and sister-in-law, about fifteen years ago. Were they ever reported missing?"

Caleb stared at Saul and went quiet for several minutes. He obviously had not expected this question. His solicitor looked at him and waited.

"They dumped the kids and went back to the continent. There was no reason to report them missing. That has nothing to do with me. I've loved those boys like my own, ask Mabel, she might know."

"Can you remember where you were when they disappeared? What area?"

"No, we travel a lot."

"All three boys were taken out of the school they were attending at the time, near Petersfield, in Hampshire. Would that be about right?"

"Yes, I remember now, they asked me to take them down to Southampton to catch the ferry over to France. I told them I would look after them. It was not Petersfield though; it was a place called Cowplain. "

"Thank you. Now may I ask, what part Elizabeth Moreby played in getting these boys for you?"

"Not much, she just did as Satan told her, too."

"Tell me, what part did the making and selling of the films you made when you raped, murdered and tortured these boys, have in your religious beliefs?"

"We needed the money, after all."

"What do you think is going to happen to you now?"

"I need help, obviously I am mentally ill. I'll go to a mental hospital."

"Have you ever tried to get help for what you have been doing, before?"

"No one would believe me. Satan said I was to tell no one."

"But what you did was wrong you must have known that?"

"Not if it was to serve him. I am special, he told me that."

"Did you not feel sorry for the boys?"

"Not really, they were chosen for me, by him."

"You said just now that you were doing this for the last ten years, what happened to start it?"

"It was Bill, I met him in prison and he got Satan to tell me."

"So, your raping and molesting your three nephews before that time were just for your sexual gratification, not the works of Satan?"

"No comment."

"And the discovery of two bodies at a traveller's site at Waterlooville near Cowplain, last year, have nothing to do with Ruth and Mark? We are getting their DNA checked now. I suspect it will come back as theirs."

"No comment."

"Tell me, why were you shunned by the travellers you had been with? Why did they cast you out?"

"That is none of your business, no comment."

"You were born a Romany. They don't allow the kind of sexual behaviour you so obviously enjoy, do they?"

"Shut up."

"I see little point in asking you any more at this time. Consult your solicitor and I will explain in a later interview the evidence I have to prove that you are not mad, just bad."

"Shut up, shut up, shut up! I'm putting a boch on you! I want to go back to my cell; I'm not saying anything more."

"By all means. I can assure you I will be questioning you again on many matters, so I think you need to have some answers that are believable ready. Interview terminated."

Outside the cell in the custody suite Saul looked at the solicitor and asked him if he was feeling ill as he looked very shaken.

"I feel rather sick, I have never heard anything like that. I'm not sure I can continue to represent him; I think I will find someone else. I'll talk to my partners in the office. What I will do, is start getting him psychologically assessed."

"I think that would be wise. Let me know if you come off the case, please. I think my colleague is throwing up in the gents, right now. Can I offer you somewhere to sit and have, maybe, a coffee? To calm yourself?"

"Thank you, but I'll get back to the office. What is a boch?"

"A gypsy curse. They only work if you believe in them. I don't,"

Saul and Paul took their time over a coffee in the canteen. Paul said, "Just how evil can someone get?"

"Very, apparently. Paul, are you all right? If it is distressing you badly, come off the squad for a while, take some leave, come back and deal with some of the many other cases we have."

"No, I just want to see him locked legally away, preferably for ever. I can cope, truly."

Once back at the office Saul looked round and he was mildly surprised at just how tidy everything was. He then went to every officer and checked their paperwork and diaries. He gave advice on and directions where needed, and then went and tidied his own office and rang Mr Owen.

"Sir, you left a note asking to talk to me?"

"I did. Can you pop down to my office now?"

"On my way."

Caroline, one of the squad, was talking to Sharon and Julia in the ladies' rest room.

"He's never done that before; checked everyone's paperwork all at once, is something up, do you think, Julia?"

"Yes, Caroline, I'm sure of it. He knows there is something about to happen. We don't have a problem normally, Sharon. We all know that if we don't get it right, we won't stay on the squad. If we have a problem, we can take it to him, or Geoff or Alan, or someone for help and it is given. We had best get back, be there if there is an inspection."

When they came in, the office was silent. Everyone but Fred, the office manager was standing. Then they saw why. There was a contingent of very senior officers looking at the paperwork and things on the desks. One of the men said, "Ah, the ladies of the team. I am Deputy Chief Constable Taylor. This is a spot check on all paperwork. Go to your desks, please, and show these officers everything."

165

The visitors found nothing wrong, much to the obvious annoyance of a couple of them. They searched every cupboard, file and register. As they were finishing, Saul walked back into the main office with Mr Owen.

"Good morning, sirs, and ma'am, can I assist you in any way?"

"Ah, Catchpole yes, I know you didn't know about our visit, but everything is so clean here, I wonder if you expected us, I cannot find anything wrong?"

"I am delighted to hear it, sir, would you care to check my office and paperwork? I'll let you in."

Saul's office had a security code lock on it, the code only being known to a very few. He and Mr Owen accompanied the DCC into the office and shut the door.

Someone whispered, "He bloody well did know, bless him!"

"Yes," said Alan, "but I think now we need to make ourselves busy. I have all the duty rotas worked out, please look at them and tell me if you need anything changed."

Alan's office was next to Saul's and it comforted him that there was just quiet conversation in Saul's office. The deputy chief constable was very strict and demanding. His visits usually ended with him finding a fault and tearing strips off the culprit. It was known he would keep looking until he found a fault. Alan worried that Saul might himself have left a small error to draw the fire of the deputy. When he heard laughter coming from Saul's office, he wondered what was going on. His own office had been checked with the main office, where he went and asked,

"Any problems with the duties, anyone? Now, listen, everyone. Please, have an overnight bag packed and be prepared to spend a few days elsewhere, on our enquiries. Those of you who have passports please include them. Anyone who speaks more than one language may be needed as we already have enquiries from abroad. All paperwork initially goes through Fred. Caroline is dealing with the families. Julia, please act up as sergeant Geoff is now acting inspector, as is Paul. Tarik, you are acting sergeant too. The governor wants to talk to all of you before you go back out, so wait, look busy and we will have our coffee when they come out."

As Saul emerged with all the other senior officers, everyone stood to attention. The deputy waved them back into their seats and said, "This is the first time, in a long series of visits, that I have been unable to find fault. It cheers me up no end. I knew Catchpole runs a tight ship. This is just one of a series of unannounced visits we are undergoing, force wide. In other departments and divisions things have not been so good, and I beseech you, if you know of anything that may bring this force into further disrepute, tell someone, someone you can trust. Loyalty to friends is not, at this time, very appropriate. Do I make myself clear?"

"Yes sir."

"Inspector, could Mr Owen borrow your office for a chat with me now? Then I think he wants to talk to you all."

"I have to go out for a short time, please, feel free."

"This way sir, how do you take your coffees, sirs?"

"White one sugar for me, how about you, Owen? White no sugar? Thank you, DC Singh, isn't it?"

Saul went down to technical services where he met Diana. They were told the cameras had been fitted in the cottage and that Gilchrist's fingerprints had been found in the two keys and the picture frame, and a DNA sample had been taken from the chip found in the locket. They were also informed that the only fingerprints found on the chip and the two keys and the picture frame were those of Gilchrist and the DNA found was being checked against his.

Meanwhile every officer in the squad saw Mr Owen and were asked if they knew or had served with a list of officers that had been suspended. Most of them did not know the officers well, or only by sight, and could tell him nothing. Then it came to Caroline's turn.

"Do you know, or have you served with any of these officers?"

He handed her a list.

"Yes, sir, two of them. Sergeant Toller, when he was a PC, and very briefly with PC Rose."

"Tell me what you know about them."

"I was at training school with Peter Toller. I didn't like him then and I don't now. He was sexist, arrogant, and lazy. He tried to make my life hell, for several reasons. He hated women, that was obvious, but he found out that I went to church, had Christian values, and he tried to belittle them and me. In the end, I just ignored him, which I think he hated most. I do remember he had at least one complaint against him then and I have heard of many others since."

"What else do you know about him?"

"He is a sympathizer of the National Front. When I first went on to CID, I was dealing with a race related intimidation case. I saw him during the course of some discreet observations on our suspect, on four occasions with National Front members. I did report it at the time, but my skipper then said it wasn't relevant to what I was doing. He also said anyone has a right to personal interests, I had the church and it was none of my business what others did in their off-duty time, providing it was legal. That skipper has since retired, for which I am very glad."

"And PC Rose?"

"He did his CID attachment with me about five years ago. He is far from bright; in fact, I have no idea how he ever got into the job. He is immature, easily led, and thought that practical jokes were an essential part of his day. I did not give him a good report, but later found his sergeant was Toller, so I was not surprised nothing happened. Then I came on the squad."

"What is your opinion of WPC Wright?"

"Nice lass, very bright, and hard working. I think she may have hidden depths. She sees what others do not always see. She is certainly an asset on the squad. May I make a comment please?"

"Certainly, if you think it will help"

"Mr Catchpole is an excellent judge of character, and so is WDC Pellow, and both of them think she is very bright indeed."

"How long have you been on this squad?"

"Four years this time, two years earlier, before I went over to Jordan on a six-month spell at the international training school there."

Tarik also knew Peter Toller. He said, "I asked to come away from his shift and complained because of his persistent racist jokes. In the short time I was on his shift two women officers resigned."

"Who did you complain to?"

"Inspector Pollock, who agreed to move me off the shift and told me it had been authorized. I was glad to get away. It was only later I found out that the complaint had gone no further than him."

"Did you try to take that further?"

"By then I had my aide to CID. It did not seem in my best interests to."

"Have you had any other racist or religious bigotry?"

"Of course I have, sir. Most of it is mindless or just ignorance. The worst was from an Afro-Caribbean colleague, who has since left the job."

"Are you talking about Garfield Hoston?"

"Yes, sir. All water under the bridge now."

"Have you had any prejudice on this squad?"

"None. It is very refreshing. We are a strange mix, from a diversity of backgrounds, cultures and educations."

"And you all get on?"

"Most of the time, yes, but if we didn't, we wouldn't last long on this squad. We need to and do work as a team."

Chapter 11

Sharon was called in next and had a long chat with Mr Owen. He was a skilful man and found out from her a lot more that she realized she knew. What impressed him was the things she did remember including dates, times, and locations.

He said, "Yes I can see what Diana means. You see and observe things almost without knowing, it is only when one puts things together that they can sometimes add up to more than their parts. Has she told you that everything is set up?"

"She rang me just now."

"I need you to tell me, and please be totally honest with me. Are you willing to act as bait in this way? There are inherent dangers to you, but I think you know that. I do not want you doing it for Catchpole, or Diana, or even the job. Are you really happy about this?"

"Yes, I am. I want to. That I have been even associated with what we think has been going on, makes my blood boil. If nothing else I will have my revenge on a horrible man who once I thought I loved. Now I see just how he used me. When we first met, he took advantage of my having lost my parents and no longer having any family. My parents were so proud when I joined up. My dad was a policeman down in London, before he retired. I suppose I thought all policemen were wonderful, but in any organization one can get bad apples. I am no longer so naïve."

When Sharon got home, she was met by Diana and Jake with Boo, who was delighted and rushed up to her and was frantically wagging her tail.

Diana suggested they walk all the dogs, so they went down to the lower meadows where the stream was. Sharon managed to totally relax for a while. Diana explained the plans to Sharon who asked, "Do you think they'll come when I'm here?"

"I'm not sure. They will not come when we are here. I've brought you down here for another reason, to show you something, that you need to know. Did you know this area is riddled with caves and old mine workings?"

"Yes, I've even been down a few caves. I rather enjoyed it."

"There is an adit down here, by the riverbank. It leads up under your cottage, all the way to the farmhouse. It was in disrepair when we came here, but we have had it fixed up. I will show you how to get in and out of it, and how to get to our house if you need to. In an emergency. Here, take this torch."

Diana led her behind a buttress of rock by a small waterfall into a small cave, from which an obviously mined tunnel ran into the hillside. They followed it some way before coming to an apparent stop.

"It goes on, round here, behind the pool of water and the waterfall. Follow me. Jake can come behind us, with the dogs."

The passageway began to rise steeply and then they came to a junction. The main passage went right, with what looked like an iron gate preventing access. Sharon looked at the latch of the gate and even opened the gate a little before closing it again.

"That's to stop any dogs or other wildlife getting in there. Bats can get in and out, but not much else. It's meant to look the main way on. It leads to the old, very unstable and dangerous mine workings. Do not go there, ever."

They went left and through a narrow slit in the rock, that Jake only just managed to squeeze himself through. They had to wait while he did so.

"We had to widen that a bit, so he could get through. I think he must have put a bit of weight on, it only took him about five minutes last time."

Jake muttered something unrepeatable and then said, "I blame your cooking."

Diana giggled. "I thought it was yours, dear, come on, we're waiting."

With a grunt and a shove Jake made it through, rubbed his stomach, and said, "I'll come down sometime and widen that, I might need to get through in a hurry."

They made their way up a narrow cave passageway, which divided. The larger passage went to the left and then round a corner. They went to the right up a passage which rose steeply up some roughly hewn steps in rock, around another rather well-hidden turning into what looked like a square chamber. It looked like a dead end, but Jake moved over to one of the corners and gently pressed it, causing the whole slab to pivot and make an entrance that it was easy to pass through. As they did so, he took Sharon's hand and put it into a small slit in the rock, where she found a small lever.

"Unless you release the lever it will not open. If you didn't know it was there, it would take ages to find it. Once inside you release it up here."

He pointed to a slightly protruding rock and showed her the lever handle behind it. They moved on up a more level passage and then came to a wooden, but quite substantial door. On it was a coded lock. Diana said, "Each of us has an individual code, so we know who has used it. It must be something Tony wouldn't even think of, what is your favourite bit of classical music? I noticed you have some good CDs of the classics; did he like them?"

"No, they actually belonged to my parents. How about 1812?"

"I'll put it in, see if it opens for you."

Once inside the door Diana put her hand up and pulled on a cord. A light came on further up a passage. There was another door and once opened it came out into the cellar of her cottage. She looked at it and saw it was disguised as a bookcase.

"I did wonder why there was a bookcase in the cellar. Two questions."

"Fire away; can we go and have a cup of tea while I explain?"

"How do I open this to get out that way, and where does the other passage go?"

"To our cellar, but your code will work for both doors. If you are under duress tap in the right code and add the letter V. That tells us where you are and that you are in need of help, and it will come. You can get out easily, just retrace our steps. I think we had better do that now, come on dogs, more walkies; no, Boo, you do not want to bring that disgusting towel with you. Have you set the video cameras on?"

"Yes, I did, but they won't see down here, will they?"

"Not in the cellar, no."

They went back into the passages and into a similar square cavity with a similar lever opener for the door Then there was a long flight of steps and another wooden door. Jake opened it and they went into a cellar with walls lined with racks of wine. Jake selected a couple of bottles as they moved up some stairs into the farmhouse hallway. Diana held up her hand for silence, as the dogs all growled softly and rushed towards the kitchen door.

Diana whispered, "Back down to the cellars! I think we have visitors."

In the main cellar there were several doors. Diana opened one that led into a warm and comfortable room which had a series of television screens on one wall. Off the room was a small kitchenette, and through another door was a small toilet.

The dogs happily went and lay on some dog beds. Sharon noticed that Mung was happily asleep on a sofa, near to a radiator.

"I thought it might be precaution to bring him here when you were not at home, just in case of this, I don't want him or Boo hurt, or you for that matter," said Diana.

They drew up chairs and watched the screens and soon saw five men approaching the cottage. They kicked the door in, Sharon gasped. "I locked that!"

Jake flicked several switches and the audio came on. They heard and saw five men in the small kitchen. They switched the light on.

Jake confirmed everything was being recorded and asked Sharon to help by identifying those she knew.

They watched and saw two men go up the stairs to her bedroom and switch the light on. One of them called out, "Yes, here it is, the picture of her beloved mother, I knew she would never get rid of it. Great, the key, good, she didn't find it. Is Vince keeping watch? We may not have long."

"Er, Tony, is it wise to put the lights on, what if one of them farmworkers sees them?"

"They'll think she has come home, that's all."

"Yes, Vince is watching. What else do we need?"

"Her photo album. That's it, over there."

"Why did you hide the keys in her stuff?"

"Because I knew she would keep them safe and no one would suspect her, she's so straight it's painful. Yes, this is the second key. Put the album back where you found it. Now we need the bank book. I wonder where she's put it?"

"I can't see anything like that."

"She's probably put it in her handbag. Look for a tan one, that's the one she uses. I just hope she hasn't looked in it."

As they watched the two men making a tidy search Sharon confirmed, "That is Tony Gilchrist and his mate Matt Buse. One of the ones in the kitchen is Damien Collins, the one in the living room is Tim Virgo and the other, I think, is Tim Mason."

"Where is your bank book, Sharon? I mean the one Mr Owen gave you to bring back"

"Under the pillow of the bed in the spare room."

"I wonder how long it will take them; they are being very tidy."

"I'm surprised. I thought Tony might want to smash things up."

"They don't want you alerted."

"Diana, look, that's him in the spare room now, yes, he's found it.

The group of men reassembled in the kitchen. Gilchrist said, "You lot go on, there is something I want to do."

"All right don't be long."

They watched as the others left, and saw Tony go to the worktop of the kitchen and take down a coffee jar from the shelf. Taking something from his pocket, he poured a powder into the coffee jar, sealed the lid, then shook the jar vigorously, before replacing it. The camera caught a very nasty, rather sly grin as he turned to leave the cottage, putting something in his pocket as he did so.

"Damn, that's a new coffee jar, I wonder what he put in it?"

"Nothing nice, certainly, we'll get it checked. He made a bad mistake; he took his gloves off to open the lid."

"Yes, and I hadn't used any coffee in the so my prints won't be on it. Do you think he wants to kill me?"

"If he did, how could he get the money? We have some spare coffee here, use that. Are you all right, lass?"

"Yes, Jake, I'm a little shaken, but very angry. What happens now?"

"We know where the safe deposit is. It's all set up. When they arrive with those keys, they'll find they do not work, and then they'll get nicked. All this is recorded. Diana is just arranging a trap for them now."

"How do we know where they're going?"

"We're tracking them. There is more to those keys than meets the eye, and the bank book. Look on this screen, three signals, all together heading towards the main road. We don't need to do much more,"

"How long has Diana been a spy?"

"A very long time. It's not quite how she would put it, but she is exceptionally good at it."

"She's very senior isn't she?"

"Yes, mainly semi-retired now, but in charge of recruitment and training."

"You do it too, and, I think, Mr Catchpole. Also, Mr Owen?"

"You catch on quick. Keep that to yourself. Now, I'll just go and get that coffee jar, then we'll relax here with some wine, or if you prefer, I have an exceptionally good brandy."

Chapter 12

DCC Owen took the call from Diana and instructed his officers. He then rang Saul. "Do you want to be in at the kill? We are about to move in. No obligation, but I wondered if you would like to be there?"

"I'd love to. Where do I meet you?"

"I'll pick you up, and I will bring a bullet proof vest and draw a firearm for you. Be ready in fifteen minutes."

"I will be. Is WPC Wright safe?"

"She is. Your DCC will be with us."

"Fine."

Saul hastily got changed and said to Anna, "Got to go out, sorry dear. I have no idea how long I will be."

"Just be careful. Please. You look like a little boy going out on an adventure! Bright eyed, bushy tailed. Please, don't get hurt."

"I'll try not to; I am only going to be observing."

"I've heard that before. Remember, I need you."

"Yes, dear, I love you, too."

Saul, Mr Owen and an inspector waited in the car while the officers got into position. Although they remained calm, there was the usual tension before a big operation. While they waited, they covered it with apparently mundane conversation.

"Saul, how long before you retire?"

"I can go in two years, but I might hang on for a bit. I like what I do and while I'm fit, I want to continue."

"I was rather hoping you would take over discipline and complaints."

"No thanks, what's wrong with Wally?"

"Nothing, he's about to be promoted to divisional commander Eastern Division. I need someone I can trust to replace him"

"Who with?"

"Well, you for a short while, until we find the right person."

"I'd hate it."

"You can go back to your beloved murder squad as soon as we have the right person."

"So, who would replace me on the squad?"

"Alan Withers, as a DCI. He's too good not to promote."

"Yes, I agree but if that happens, I want another couple of promotions as well."

"Who?"

"Geoff Bickerstaff as DI, Julia Pellow as DS and Paul Christie to DI on division. I'd like Tarik Singh made up, too. They're all qualified but won't leave the squad. Paul needs divisional experience, but I'll have him back any time. I want Sharon Wright on the squad too, she's very bright."

Mr Owen said, "Well, you can't have her for long, she's going to Special Branch very soon."

Saul said, "So you're asking me to run two departments, complaints and discipline, and also oversee the murder squad?"

"I suppose I am, yes."

"It's a lot of hard work and is hardly likely to make me popular."

"Well, unless you can find someone from another force who can take over from Wally."

"I'll think on it. It looks like something is about to happen."

They watched as a car pulled up further down the road and three men got out and walked back towards the building where the safe deposit lockers were kept. They rang the doorbell to let themselves in. What they did not know was the place was already set up with cameras and there were officers secreted in there already, waiting for them. Saul and his two companions quickly got out of their car and went round the side of the building where the manager was waiting to let them in. They went to his office through another door. There they watched on several screens, while the three men made their way to the section where their safe deposit was secured.

Once there Tony Gilchrist and two others put their large bags on the floor and emptied them, bringing out more bags. All of which seemed empty. Tony smiled and said, "Right, remember, as soon as we have it, back to your place, Vince, we share it out and then get out of the country. I'm flying out from Manchester this evening."

"I'm booked on a ferry from Liverpool," said Vince, "and Al here is taking the Eurostar to Paris. What's the matter? Lock sticking?"

Tony tried the second key, but that did not work either.

"The keys don't work. Let's call the manager; they must have changed all the locks."

The manager, together with Saul and several other officers and Mr Owen came into the corridor. Mr Owen said, "No, the keys won't work. You're all under arrest for robbery and perverting the course of justice."

Gilchrist stared at them for a few seconds, obviously recognizing Saul, and said, "You bastard, you're behind all this!"

Saul smiled saying, "True, now come on, gentlemen. This is the end of the line for you, give up."

Gilchrist stepped back and pulled a small pistol from his pocket and pointed it at Saul.

"Let us go or I'll shoot. I have nothing to lose now."

Saul ducked behind the steel containers as other officers armed with larger guns made their presence felt. Gilchrist's two companions dithered for a moment and then took shelter, leaving him standing alone.

"Gilchrist, there's no way out." One of the firearms officers said, "You have ten seconds to drop the gun, or we will shoot."

About three seconds later Gilchrist dropped the gun and lay down on his front with his arms out, totally surrendering. The other two men immediately gave themselves up. They were searched and were found to be carrying loaded firearms. These were disarmed. Whilst they watched, cuffed, and waiting to go to a prison van, the correct keys were produced and the lock-up was opened. Inside storage boxes revealed huge wads of banknotes, some police equipment, firearms, a box of bearer bonds, correspondence including bank statements for banks both in the United Kingdom and Switzerland, mobile phones, and some pretty sophisticated electronic equipment, including taser guns.

"Aladdin's cave!" said Saul, "Tell me Gilchrist, what was it you put in Sharon's coffee at her cottage?"

"I don't know what you mean."

"Yes, you do. It's being analysed as we speak."

"Pity the little slut didn't drink it."

"Well, she didn't. What was it?"

"Just something to make her regret throwing me over. All right, an emetic to make her ill."

"Where did you get it from?"

"I've a mate who's a chemist."

"Who? "

"None of your business."

Saul looked at Gilchrist in front of him and drew breath.

"What happened to turn you from a police officer, into a criminal?"

"Money and what it could get me. It's people like you, with no imagination, who can never understand. If it is there, you are a fool to turn it down. The country is going to the dogs anyway. All values have gone. We're welcoming immigrants whose own countries don't even want them, and if you don't take what is there, you're a fool. I reckon the Nazis had the right idea about your sort."

"Even in prison?"

"It was a risk worth taking. If you had not interfered, I'd be sunning myself on a beach by now. You've made life very difficult for me, so watch your back. If I can get my revenge on you, I will."

"How is threatening me, going to go make life easier for you?"

"It will make me feel better, knowing you can never relax. You may have got me, but not all of my friends. When I do get out, I'll come looking for you, believe it. It's what will keep me going."

"You sad man. Your threats don't worry me. If I'm still alive when you finally get out, if you ever do, I shall look forward to putting you back in a cell. Meanwhile, I shall enjoy my life in freedom, which you won't. Take him away!"

For the next two hours items were bagged up, labelled and taken to secure premises, where they could be forensically examined, and evidential copies of tapes were obtained.

Mr Owen took Saul aside. "Saul, his threats worry me. I think you should be careful."

"If I am still alive when he gets out, I will have a zimmer frame. Now what else do you need me to do here?"

"It's all in hand. I'll get someone to run you home."

"Don't bother. I'll get a taxi or a bus."

"No, I don't think so. I'm told that every time you break free on your own, you run into trouble,."

"That's not fair!"

"Maybe. You fall across trouble without even trying. I'll drop you off."

Saul arrived home and after a light meal he went into the living room and resumed a painting he was doing. Anna looked across at him and remarked, "Something is worrying you. Can I help?"

"I doubt it, they're trying to co-opt me to take over complaints and discipline for a while, until they find someone else, as Wally is being promoted."

"How long for?"

"Not long, they need to find the right person. I could retire, it isn't like we need the money."

"Well, don't decide tonight. Come on let's head to bed. You look very tired."

After Saul had left the next morning, Anna rang Diana.

"Di, can we talk"

"Sure, your place or mine?"

"Neither. I'll meet you in town."

"One o clock then. See you there."

Anna arrived early and waited. Diana was, as expected, on time.

"Obviously, it's about Saul. What's up?"

Anna explained about the threatened posting to complaints and discipline and said, "He doesn't want this, but they're trying to press him to do it. He's talking about retiring, it will destroy him."

"I see that. He needs to do what he does so very well. Do you want me to talk to him?"

"No, not unless he comes to you. What do I do?"

"You have done it, told me. I think I might know the very person for the job. Leave it with me."

"Thanks, Di, have you time for some retail therapy?"

"Always. Let's hit the shops, big time!"

Chapter 13

Saul waited at the traffic lights, in a queue of cars on his way into work. It was the usual rush hour snarl up of city traffic. Ahead of him was a lilac coloured Picasso, with three children in the back. The lights turned to green and he moved cautiously forward, following the car in front. Behind him was a large truck. It was a big junction, and as they all slowly moved forwards a red car came screaming towards them from their right. It had not only jumped the lights but was travelling far too fast to stop. Saul braked and came to a halt. The red car tried to squeeze between him and the Picasso, but swerved violently and hit the Picasso, and then with a loud crash hit Saul's car and flew up into the air, landing on its roof, and with a screech of metal crunched itself into the front of the truck behind him. Saul called for help on his phone, switched the engine off, grabbed the first aid kit from his car, and a blanket, and tried to open his driver's door. The window had been shattered as has had the windscreen. He climbed out of his car via the back door and went first to the Picasso. People had rushed from all points to help. There was a man attending to the family in the Picasso, who said he was a doctor. Saul went to the red car and peered in. He saw movement inside the crumpled body of the car. The truck driver joined him, despite pouring blood from a head wound. He said, "You all right, mate?"

"I think so. Here, help me."

Together they helped a young woman out of the car, who was then taken by some other helpers to the pavement. She was cut and crying, and obviously had an injured arm. The driver, a young man, was unconscious but breathing. He was trapped so Saul did not try to move him, but checked his that airway was clear and made a collar for his neck out of the blanket. He heard the woman scream about a baby and after removing the keys from the ignition, crawled into the back seat of the car and found a toddler strapped into a child's car seat. The truck driver loaned him a penknife, and together they managed to cut the seat and the child out of the car. By this time, the doctor had come from the Picasso and Saul beckoned him to attend the driver.

Saul picked up his first aid kit and said to the truck driver, "Thanks for that. Here let me patch you up."

Saul looking around, said, "What a mess!"

The truck driver nodded. "There was nothing we could do. Is he dead, in the red car?"

"I don't think so. He's breathing. Do you hurt anywhere else?"

"My foot is a bit sore. How about you?"

"A couple of bruises, I think, I'd best check the other family."

"I'll come with you."

The family from the Picasso were shaken, bruised, with a few cuts, but remarkably uninjured. The driver, a woman in her forties, asked, "What about the other car, the red one?"

"We got the woman and baby out; the doctor is with the driver now."

"Where did he come from? I never saw him until there was this huge bang."

"Over there, he jumped the lights. It was not your fault. I was in the Saab behind you."

"Shouldn't we be exchanging details or something?"

"The police will sort all that, they shouldn't be long. I'll give you my card anyway."

Saul took out his wallet and handed the woman and the truck driver his card. The truck driver said, "You're a policeman?"

"Yes, I am. The fire brigade has arrived, and there is the ambulance, and the police are here now."

The junction was soon full of the emergency services, and while the paramedics and fire brigade saw to the red car, Saul went to the mother and small child.

"Is the child all right?"

"Yes, thank you so much for what you did. I'm so sorry. It was Mark's fault. Thanks for getting me and little Dale out. You're hurt!"

"Not badly. I've had worse."

Saul looked around at the scene and then found a traffic sergeant who seemed to be in charge.

"I was the driver of the green Saab. I'm also a police officer. What can I do to help?

"Yes, sir, I know who you are. If you want to help, go the hospital with the others, after we have got the trapped driver out."

Saul pointed out the other drivers and said, "I don't think I need medical attention; I'm not hurt."

"Which is why there is a cut on your ear, you have a large lump on your forehead, and obviously a fairly serious cut above your elbow which still seems to be bleeding?"

Saul looked at his right arm and saw the blood oozing out of a torn sleeve of his jacket. He suddenly realized that it did hurt.

"I didn't notice. All right, if it makes you happy, but I will need my briefcase and laptop from my car. It looks a write off. Can you get it taken to the Saab dealers at Headingly?"

"Of course."

"Until we get carted off, what can I do to help?"

"You can provide me with a specimen of breath, please?"

"Certainly, now?

" Yes. Come and sit in the traffic car."

As Saul expected, he showed no trace of alcohol and neither did the truck driver. The woman driver showed a faint trace. She said, "I had a glass of wine last night, but I wasn't drunk."

The police officer taking her sample said, "No, madam, you are well below the permitted level. Now, all of you, please go in the ambulance. The other driver has been cut free and is already on his way. We'll catch up with you at the hospital."

The truck driver, the family from the Picasso and Saul, made their way to the waiting ambulance.

At the hospital Saul waited patiently for his turn to be seen, fully accepting that he was not badly injured. Sat waiting with him were the family from the Picasso and the truck driver. Saul was seen by a triage nurse who cleaned up, stitched and dressed the cuts, on his arm and his ear, and sent him off to x-ray for the now considerable bump on his forehead to be checked. Resigned to a lengthy wait, he sat in the queue and thought about the problem of being sent to take over the complaints and discipline department. He was x-rayed and sent back to A&E and soon the truck driver was sitting beside him.

"You're going to have a couple of good black eyes there, mate."

"I know. The silly thing is it doesn't even hurt. How about you?"

"A couple of stitches in the cut on my head, and they think I've a broken a metatarsal bone in my foot. Hey, do you fancy a cuppa?"

"Good idea. I know where the machine is, I'll get it. What would you like?"

Saul came back with a drink for both of them and they sat together, idly chatting. After a while, the traffic sergeant appeared and said to Saul, "Can I catch up with you at your home, sir, later?"

"By all means; but I might be in my office, I have work to do."

"I know where to find you."

Saul was called in to see the duty doctor who took one look at him and said, "Not you, again! Been fighting? Really, at your age!"

"Not this time, it was a road traffic accident and not my fault."

"I thought senior officers of your exalted rank didn't get out and about much, at least they kept out of the fracas."

Saul smiled wryly."So did I! I was just in the wrong car at the wrong time."

The doctor examined him and did some simple tests and then said, "Were you the one who stabilized the neck of the other driver?"

"Yes, with a rolled-up blanket, it was all I could do. How is he?"

"Thanks to you, he will probably walk again. You saved his spine, if not his life. He has a broken neck, but because you did the right thing he may recover. Thanks for that. Now, you don't have any fractures. Did you lose consciousness?"

"No, I'm fine."

"Then go home. I don't need to keep you in, this time."

As Saul left the A&E department the truck driver was hobbling out, his foot in plaster. Saul held the door open for him and said, "Is someone picking you up?"

"No, I'll have to get a taxi. My boss is dealing with the truck, but I need to get to the depot and pick my gear up. He says he'll take me home from there. How about you?

"I need to get a taxi. Where do you need to go?"

"Kent Street."

"Just round the corner from my station. I'll get a taxi and drop you off."

Saul rang a taxi firm and as they waited, they sat on a wooden bench. The truck driver said, "My name is Pete Clark. Are you not the detective dealing with all those child murders? I think I saw your appeal on the telly. I've been trying to place where I'd seen you before."

"Yes, I am, my name is Saul."

"Yes, I read it on the card. Look, I might have some information for you, to do with those missing kids. I was going to come forward, but it's so, well, sort of disconnected, I didn't want to waste anyone's time. I don't know if I would just be clouding the issue. Who do I tell?"

"Me. Tell me what has been bugging you?"

"All right. I work long haul mostly. I do a regular run, carrying furniture down the A1 to Cambridgeshire.

Me and another driver, we tend to take turns with it. I always stop for a break on the way back at a transport café some miles from where I get back onto the A1. So does the other driver. There is sometimes a travellers' camp next to it. Some weeks back I had to take his turn and pulled in there, got a mug of coffee, and when I got back to my lorry, this traveller was waiting for me. He said, 'Where's Robert?' I explained he had gone sick. The chap was really annoyed and said, 'Well, he was going to drop something off for me. Have you got it?' I looked through the cab and found an envelope addressed to Caleb, which is what this man said his name was. I told the man to wait and rang Robert at his home. He said to give the man the envelope and to keep quiet about it. I looked in the envelope and saw a lot of pictures from a computer, mainly of a boy. I didn't think any more of it, gave the chap the envelope and I went back there the next week, which was my turn, and again I went to the café. I asked about the travellers; they said they'd gone. I got the impression the lady in the café didn't like them much. While I was there, I saw a poster up on the wall about a missing boy and it looked a bit like the kid in the photos, in the envelope. I asked Robert when I got back. He said no, it was pictures of his nephew. But the more I think, the more I'm sure it was the missing kid. Then I heard you had arrested a chap called Caleb; it's not a common name. I was going to ring, but it is not even in the same part of the country."

"Can you remember when this was?"

"A while back, maybe two, three months. I can check in the lorry's logbook."

"Who is this Robert?"

"He calls himself Robert Galliver. He's a strange chap. I don't like him much, he's not been with us long, a year maybe. He gives me the creeps, actually. I don't know much about him. He's single and lives on his own. All I really know is that he can't drive on the first Monday of the month, he has some sort of appointment he cannot break. Shall I find out his address?"

"Please do. Where did he live before?"

"Nottingham, I think. Shall I ring you?"

"If you would. There's a missing boy outstanding, from Cambridgeshire, called Nathan Cox, eleven years old. He's been missing nearly four months."

"That's the name on the poster, I remember now. I know this sounds cowardly, but if Robert knew I was speaking to you about this, he might get really nasty. He has told several of us to mind our own business, if we asked anything, personal like. I do know something about him, not what he told me."

"What?"

"He goes down to Newmarket a lot. He says to the races, but he does not. The days he goes are not race days, I know because my cousin is a bookie. I've a work mate who is mad keen on archaeology, and he's at some sort of voluntary dig at a place called Devil's Dyke, just outside Newmarket, a place called Wooditton, near a village called Saxon Street. He saw Robert there several times in the woods, with a load of travellers, but Robert hadn't clocked him. My mate said they were going to start on the dig one morning. He saw Robert and three travellers, all men, coming out of the woods further up the track, and it looked like they didn't want anyone to see them. They were muddy; looked like they'd been digging. My mate is quite a short feller and he admitted he sort of hid behind one of the taller chaps, because he don't like Robert and is, I think, a bit scared of him, but he told me."

"Leave it with me. Find out what you can, discreetly, and we can meet up for a drink."

"Sure, do you know the Nags Head, down from my depot?"

"I do. Shall we meet there?"

"Yes, in the saloon bar. I'll ring you."

Chapter 14

When Saul got into the office, Alan Withers looked at him and said, "Should you be here? They rang through to say you were delayed because of an accident, but not that you were in it."

"Yes, I should. Can you get me the file on Nathan Cox?"

"The lad from Cambridge? Yes, sure. Have you got something?"

"I think so. Please also check on a Robert Galliver, used to live in Nottingham area but now lives in Leeds. Find out if he is signing on somewhere on the first Monday of the month. He's a lorry driver."

"Will do. Is your car irreparably damaged?"

"I think it's a write off. I must ring my insurance and get a replacement, I should also ring my wife, she's not going to be pleased."

Saul arranged a loan car, and had spoken to Anna, and was catching up on paperwork when their deputy chief constable, Mr Taylor, walked in, waved him back to his seat, sat down in the chair opposite and said, "I just heard about the crash. It seems you did some excellent first aid, well done. What I want to know, is how, whenever you move out of the office on your own, you come across mayhem?"

"That's not strictly true, sir."

"Fair enough. The reason I'm here is, however, is to tell you that you have friends in high places. It seems that I will not be needing you in discipline and complaints just yet. I have been offered a first-class officer who can start right away. I have been told, quite emphatically, that you need to stay just where you are."

"I have no idea what you're talking about, I haven't spoken to anyone."

"Well, it doesn't matter. The chap they've offered us will make a good job. Now, it looks like you need to be heading home; you're covered in blood, have a massive bruise all over your face and a torn jacket. Go home, that is an order!"

"Yes, sir, but I have to do something rather important first. I picked up some good information that needs urgent action. I'm waiting on some more coming in now."

"Then do it, then go home. You look ghastly!"

"Do I? Is this just at the moment, or generally?"

"Now, not generally, you clot. Have you actually looked in a mirror?"

"No. Is it that bad?"

"Yes, you can't work like that. While we're waiting, I want to talk to you about something else. About when you were threatened. I want you to have an alarm at your place, and you are to carry one."

"If I got twitchy at every threat, I'd be a bag of nerves. I get threats a lot because I deal with the scum of the earth. Even Caleb James tried to put a gypsy curse on me."

"Does that worry you?"

"No. They only work if you believe in them, I don't."

"Nevertheless, I want a degree of protection for you. And if it restricts your activities, you will have to live with it."

"If you say so, sir. Ah, the email I'm expecting, excuse me."

The deputy watched as Saul read it through and he then said, "What you expected?"

"More than I hoped for. I think I need to visit Cambridge. We may have traced another missing boy."

"Then get Withers to deal with it. He is more than capable. I'm serious, Saul, you *will* have some time off."

"Yes, I suppose he could, I do need to meet an informant, however."

"Then do it and get home. Hand over to Withers and then take that lovely wife of yours for a week's holiday, but I would like to know where you are."

As soon as the deputy had gone, Saul busied himself, making it easier for Alan to take over. The traffic sergeant came and took a statement from him. He explained that the driver of the red car was way over the drink drive limit, so would in due course be prosecuted, and was likely to make an almost full recovery. Before he left, the traffic sergeant said, "Sir, I want to thank you, not only for what you did today, but for exposing Gilchrist. I never liked him and was never happy with his work and was glad when he went over to another jurisdiction. He knew I was on to him and made sure I never had an excuse to catch him out. Most of my colleagues think the same and we are thankful for what you did."

Saul finished explaining everything to Alan, and then took a call from the truck driver. After a brief chat on the phone, Saul said, "I'll be back, I need to meet someone."

In the Nag's Head, he found Peter Clark and joined him, with a drink for both of them. Peter said, as he handed him an address, "I've remembered something else. Robert is not a tidy chap. I cleared the cab on one occasion and found a bottle of chloroform in there, almost empty. He snatched it from me, saying that it was used to destroy vermin and to mind my own business. It seemed strange at the time."

After a genial chat, Saul walked back to the office, met Alan, and handed over all the information and checked he had all he needed. He then took a taxi, picked up his personal things from his wrecked car at the yard and was taken home.

As he entered his home, Anna met him and handed him a drink and made him sit down.

"Bed, now! You look grey. Don't tell me that you're fine, because I don't believe it. Have a shower and get some rest. I'll take any calls and deal with them."

"Thank you. I must admit, I've had better days. Just the after-effects of the accident, I expect."

"Not to mention not enough sleep and worrying about your proposed posting."

"Yes. Who did you speak to?"

"I just mentioned it to Diana, I asked her advice."

"That explains it then. I'm not, thankfully, being posted any more. I have been ordered to take a week's leave. I'll just ring the Worms Head Hotel and book it."

"How wonderful! I do love it at Rhossilli, and the Gower. I'll pack."

Sharon felt relaxed and relieved, and for the first time in months, safe, when Mr Owen told her that Gilchrist and all his known cronies were locked up. He visited her in the cottage to give her an update, and said, "We have found out what he put in your coffee; it was most unpleasant. He's been charged with that as well. I have some paperwork to go through with you, mainly bank authorisations, and we need a supplementary statement, but then I think until the trial you can get your life back on track. Are you going to stop here for a while?"

"Yes, I spoke to Diana, we agreed a sum for the rent, too little, I think. I love it here. Now I have the dog it's ideal. Sir, may I suggest you don't leave your briefcase there, she's far too interested in it. She's already chewed one of my older handbags. I like helping with the animals as well. I am learning a great deal."

Mr Owen rescued his briefcase in the nick of time, and after a little while was able to return to his office, to continue putting the huge file together.

Chapter 15

Two months later, it was very obvious that Caleb did not like being in prison. He had not been there long when he discovered that he was hated and despised, by prisoners and staff alike. Always before he had manged to survive by threats, bullying and if necessary, violence. But this time he discovered he was a small fish in a big pond. No one wanted to take his side. Within a week he had requested to be removed from the general prison population and was sent to another wing.

He had done his best when being examined and assessed by several shrinks. He had been so sure he would convince them that he was mentally ill and not responsible for what he did. All but one had seen through him, his new solicitor had told him that. He didn't really like his new solicitor very much; he was cold and efficient and very proper. He had met his barrister and had been told what to expect when he went to court.

Caleb had tried to contact Cain, Seth, Mabel and the rest of his family, but had received nothing back. He needed to think of a new method of getting out of his situation.

Cain and Seth had done likewise and were resigned to a spell in prison, and each of them had taken the opportunity to improve their education there. Petunia, or Mary as she was now known, was having a tough time in the de-tox centre. Fear of what might happen to her outside was all that kept her there, but as her mind began to clear, and her body responded to a drug free, healthy diet, she felt physically and mentally better. She remembered things more clearly and wrote down everything. When Reuben sent her a message, passed on through the police, she was almost relieved when he said he would not be contacting her again. Their relationship was over. He had wished her luck and thanked her for the good times they had shared.

Reuben took his caravan and her old van, and headed over the continent, ending up in the Dordogne. There was enough tourist trade to sell quite a lot of his artwork. In the van, when he was looking for something else, he found a forgotten sculpture of hers, which he sold. Suffering from an unaccustomed attack of conscience, he sent the money to the murder squad office to be given to her.

By sheer coincidence, Tony Gilchrist was put on the same remand wing as Caleb. They were seated near to each other watching the television, when a news clip reviewed the progress of the child disappearances and Saul's press conference at the start of the investigation was shown briefly. Simultaneously, both swore and yelled abuse at the television.

Caleb looked at Tony and asked, "Why do you hate him?"

"He put me here. The bastard. If I can ever do him harm, I will. "

"We need to talk then. I hate him too."

Their friendship, such as it was, was a strange one. Staff and prison officers were amazed when they saw the two of them, often talking together. The officers suspected there was a sinister motive behind it and recorded what they could of meetings the two men had.

Tony Gilchrist had also found his so-called friends had deserted him. As a police officer, in prison he had been immediately put on a wing separate from the main prison population for his own protection. His only visitors had been his parents. When they had told him they wanted nothing more to do with him he realized he had no friends left. His sister had written to him, returning his visiting order, and saying she would not be supporting him. His next step was trying to get the several crooks and in one case, a gang leader he had worked for, to help him, but they turned their backs on him and sent a message saying if he implicated them he would not live long. He was attacked in the showers one day and beaten up as a message to that effect.

His only friend was Caleb, who railed on about Saul Catchpole, so together they plotted their escape. It almost filled their waking hours and was all that gave them hope.

Caleb was interviewed again, this time by Detective Sergeant Paul Christie, about more bodies that had been found. He had declined a solicitor and told prison staff he had nothing to say but the interview was quite a lengthy one, mainly, they thought, for him to vent his spleen at the police. Paul had emerged from the interview remarkably unscathed and said all he had done was to listen, in the hopes he might learn something useful. Paul returned a few days later to clarify a few matters, when Caleb seemed quite happy to talk to him.

Following the information about Galliver and Devil's Dyke, Alan Withers assisted the Cambridgeshire Police and officers from Suffolk in the recovery of four bodies from the woods at Devil's Dyke, one of which was identified as Nathan Cox.

Robert Galliver was arrested and interviewed. He was found to be a known sex offender. He had been picked up when he reported at his local police station on the first Monday of the month. When questioned about the disappearance of Nathan Cox, faced with a mass of forensic evidence, he spilled his guts and provided the police with more evidence and the location of several more bodies.

Alan Withers and the team were kept very busy. Alan very soon realized that there was a lot of work that he was unaware of, that was usually done by Saul.

Meanwhile, Saul and Anna were having another very relaxing holiday on the beautiful Gower peninsula, enjoying walks on the cliffs and the beaches. Saul was happy to sit and paint, and Anna was knitting garments for the impending new grandchild. She knew him well enough to know that he needed to calm down and had been very worried about the cases he was handling. She thought back to other holidays they had enjoyed, and each time he had come away from them more relaxed and yet more focused on what to do. For two days their son and daughter-in-law, and grandchild, Benjamin, came to join them, and they had a wonderful time on the beach as the weather was fine. When they left, Anna drove back, and Saul seemed ready to return to work, which he did the following day. It took him another two days to catch up on all the enquires and he realized just how hard his team had worked and how much he relied on them.

On the third day, Julia Pellow knocked on his door and said, "Sir, thank you."

"Whatever for?"

"My promotion. I get made up next week, but on this squad. I know you recommended me."

"Only what you deserve. How's Sharon doing?"

"Fine, we make a very good team. She's out with Tarik on a follow up enquiry. He wants to thank you, too, as does Geoff. We're throwing a joint promotion celebration party on Friday evening, all of us, and we want you there. Paul has had to take some leave, some family matter, but said he will thank you when he gets back."

"Where is this party then?"

"Police Club, eight o'clock."

"I'd love to, but I don't want to cramp your style?"

"You won't!"

Saul smiled and said, "Things are moving on, Julia. The squad will need to expand if we're to follow up all these enquiries. If you, or any of the others, can think of any officer who is up to being a squad member, if only for a while, please let me know."

The next day there was a list of names on his desk when he got there. As usual he was one of the first in and was quickly followed by his sergeant, Geoff Bickerstaff. Together they visited several stations, talking to some of those who had been recommended. Just before lunch they caught up with one officer, Simon Hart. That he was young, capable and efficient was clear from his excellent record. They found him in the CID office; Geoff introduced them and said, "Have you time for a break?"

"Not really. I must get this file together before I go today."

Saul picked up the file and said, "This is complicated. Talk me through it as you work and if I can help I will."

The file was one for a case of blackmail. Together the three of them sorted it out and put it together. Saul looked at the summary, commented, "This must have taken hours to do. Who helped you?"

"No one, sir. I tend to work alone. It did take a long time. I solved the case by observation, watching where the money was left. The others in the office thought I was wasting my time."

"Do you not get on with them?"

"Yes and no. There is no antagonism, but they think I'm a bit strange. I don't drink, don't swear and I don't socialise very much."

"Why?"

"I'm a Mormon. I don't think they approve."

"I see. If you came on my squad you would have to fit in, work as part of a team."

"I know and I would like to. Your squad has a reputation of being unprejudiced; tolerant of different lifestyles."

"I hope so. If you came on the squad, could you give it the hours it needs?"

"Yes, willingly. I have nothing against the others here, but they don't include me in some of their social things, because, I think, they think I might judge them. It's not my place to do so."

"Judge not and ye shall not be judged? You have excellent reports from your line managers."

He was, as usual one of the first in, and saw Geoff coming in behind him. The two of them spent the morning visiting several stations, talking to officers and assessing how suitable they might be. One officer who had been recommended and had applied on a previous occasion was a Simon Hart.

"They know I put the work in. I get results."

"Do you want to come on my squad?"

"I should be honoured to do so."

"Then report to my office on Monday morning."

"Thank you, sir. Before you go, I think you might be interested in something I heard."

"Go on."

"Tony Gilchrist and Caleb Jones are both on remand in the same prison. One of the wardens there is a member of my church and a friend. He told me the two of them are palled up and plotting something. They both, apparently, hate you and have several times mentioned they would like to kill you. I thought you should know"

"That is interesting. Do we know how they intend to do this?"

"No. He thinks they're plotting to escape. He has told the prison authorities who suggested that it's just talk. They say they have informed the police. I served with Gilchrist once and I know him. I didn't like him, but I do know he has a devious and clever mind."

"Yes, I got that impression. Thanks for the warning. Is there anyone else you think might contribute to the squad?

"Yes, but I wonder if he is too young in service."

"Who?"

"Mario Verdi. He has just done an aide to CID here. We worked together rather well. He's a nice lad, very astute. He reads people very well. He's on shift downstairs now. He also speaks several languages. He is, I think, originally from Malta. He's a bit of a loner as well, because he's a devout Catholic."

Saul and Geoff went to the cell block to find Verdi. The custody sergeant looked up as they entered stood to attention and said, "Hello, sir, good to see you. What brings you here?"

"Paddy, since when has it been, sir? Surely, we know each other well enough to still be on first name terms?"

"Thanks, Saul, I was only being polite. Caught any good warthogs recently?"

"One or two. How are you and your family?"

"Fine. I'm looking forward to retiring next month. I was going to ask you to my farewell do. I'm trying to get a civilian job in admin somewhere. How is Anna and that brat pack of yours? I hear you have a massive case on."

"Stephen and Samuel have left home, both married. I am a grandfather. The girls are doing very well at their school. I'm trying to recruit staff for the squad, some temporary, some not. Don't suppose you would be interested as deputy office manager under Fred Dunlop?"

"Yes, very. May I suggest someone, Simon Hart?"

"Already on board as from Monday. Can I talk to Verdi?"

"Yes, he'd be good too. Both fine chaps."

"Paddy, will you start on Monday as well? There's a condition though,"

"What?"

"You don't tell too many people about the many mistakes I made when we were on shift together?"

"I will make no promises. Here's Verdi now. You know who this is, Mario?"

"Yes, I do."

"PC Verdi, do you want an aide to CID?"

"Very much sir."

"On the murder squad?"

"That's my ultimate dream I think, sir."

"Then come Monday morning with Hart and O'Grady here. We parade at nine."

About fifteen minutes later they headed back to the Squad room. Saul explained to Geoff, "Paddy was my tutor constable when I first joined. Great bloke with a wicked sense of humour. His best talent is organising things."

When they got back to the office Saul made some lengthy calls to personnel and then returned to the main office. Saul called all those in the offices together and told them of the expected new additions to the squad. More desks were obtained from the stores and things were made ready. Saul called Alan Withers into his office.

"Is Paul all right? I heard he had to take leave because of a family problem?"

"To be honest, I don't know," Alan replied. "I have tried to ring him at his home several times. His mobile is switched off. He said something about a grandmother, and a funeral, so maybe he's sorting that out."

"I thought he did that last year, but maybe it's his other grandmother. He is a rather private chap so I would not want to intrude. We'll try later."

On the Friday morning, Saul got a lift from Anna rather than take his new car into town and leave it there. He suspected he might have a bit too much to drink at the party later on. He had not actually driven the new car yet, as he wanted to properly acquaint himself on a rest day. It had been parked on his drive for four days. He had been to promotion parties before and knew that they could get lively, to say the least. He spent the day getting everything neat and tidy in his and the main office as he suspected another inspection was imminent. He also made a point of having a substantial tea in the canteen, before heading to the party. It was a very happy affair. His speech produced much laughter. He had sat down again and was contemplating a third glass of wine, when his bleeper went off. He always carried it, even when off duty, except for the times he was on holiday. He went into a nearby office and rang the control room.

A few minutes later he returned to the party and spoke to Alan Withers, whose bleeper had also just gone off, and the asked for the music to be turned down.

"Sorry to spoil the fun, folks, but I thought you should know Caleb Jones and Tony Gilchrist escaped from prison in the last three hours. I will have to leave you to it. Carry on unless you need to do something."

There was a mass exodus back to the office and no one wanted to go home. Saul was about to go out on an enquiry when the chief constable walked in with two armed officers.

"No, Saul. You have a guard. Your wife is already being protected, she's been taken to a safe place where you will be joining her. You are their probable target. The rest of you get directions from control room. WPC Wright and Mr Catchpole, please go with these officers now."

Saul and Sharon were hurried into a nearby office. Saul said to the chief, "Are you sure this is necessary?"

"Yes, very. Both of you put body armour on. We'll take you to the farm. It's all set up and you'll be safe there. Your sister-in-law knows and it is all prepared."

"You think they'll try to get Sharon?"

"It's possible. If they do try, we'll be ready for them."

"How did they get out?"

"We think in the laundry van. It has disappeared. We're searching for it now."

"Did they have help?"

"We think so. Now, get what you need and go with these officers. Now!"

Saul was issued with a firearm. He and Sharon were then bundled into the back of a large van and driven up to Diana and Jake's, where they were waiting for them.

Anna was sitting in their lounge, placidly knitting baby garments.

"Are you all right, darling? I'm so sorry about all this."

"Yes, dear, fine. I've been prepared for days. The chief explained to me when he came to see me earlier in the week. He said you would not worry about it, so he had to. Now, I'm going to sit quietly with Sharon here while you talk to Diana and Jake. All the dogs have been walked, her cat is safe, as are the dogs. I've prepared sandwiches and coffee for everyone."

Saul looked at his wife in amazement. There was no doubt she was totally in control of the situation which, he had to admit, he wasn't. He went into the kitchen and found Diana and asked her, "So now what do we do?"

"We wait. It may interest you to know that your car outside your house, had a bomb planted under it. When did you last use it?"

"I haven't yet."

"Don't worry, it was easily diffused. Very simple, no booby-traps, so I'm told. Your neighbours said there was a group of travellers in the road this morning."

"Who?"

"From the description, Mabel and some of her gang. We had several of them hanging round in the village and up the lane here last week, but they never got close enough. I expect them here, soon. They know a lot about you. Is there anyone on your team you don't trust?"

"No. You think we've been betrayed?"

"I think you have, certainly. Someone who knows where you will go, and where you live."

"I'd trust any of my team."

"I would not. I think I know, but we'll have to let the game play itself out. I've no proof. There is more to this than we think. I need you to think carefully who was in the paedophile list…"

"You mean the recipients of the porn videos?"

"Yes, and who might want to silence Jones."

"I didn't deal with that, Paul said he would do that."

"Yes. Where is he, back at the party?"

"No, he couldn't come, he has a family emergency and has been away on leave."

"Anyone else conspicuous by their absence?"

"Nita knew she had a something planned. I think it was her sister's wedding, and one of our newer members, Sean, he was playing football."

"Really? What is his surname?

"Hopkins."

"Was there a Hopkins on that list?"

"Yes, but it was down in the West Country, an apparently respectable school master. Near Wells, I think."

"Who investigated it?"

"Paul, before he went on leave. He wrote it up."

"How long have you known Paul?"

"He's been with me quite a few years, about five, I think. Totally reliable, very correct, good at the paperwork side of things and a rather quiet, but pleasant chap. I do know he cares deeply for child welfare."

"Has it occurred to you that Jones may have been sprung to get revenge on him?"

"No, it hadn't. Diana how could I get it so wrong?"

"You didn't. You can only act on what you know or suspect. It may be nothing like that. Who else hates you?"

"Loads of people, most of them locked up."

"Did you know Toller had gone missing?"

"I didn't even know he had got bail."

"He was on bail and failed to sign on two days ago."

"Why was I not told?"

"You're no longer dealing with it, Owen is. You have your hands full already."

"What can I do now?"

"Wait. Incidentally, I can tell you that you can trust Sharon. Anna is talking to her now, finding out a couple of things."

"Why Anna? She should not be involved. I won't have my wife dragged into this."

"She's been on board for a lot longer than you realise. She's just finding out something for me."

"That you or I could not?"

"Yes. Sharon sees things, notices them. Things maybe you would not. I call it joining the dots. You're good at it, but here, you're too close to see. I think I might be as well. Anna is not."

"I've always tried to shield her from parts of my job."

"She knows that. Which is why, now, she's just the right person."

"Is it me they're trying to kill?"

"Yes, but Sharon too, and they won't hesitate if they get the chance. I'm sorry Saul, but we put a trace on your phone in your house when you were away. Anna agreed. It has come up with something interesting."

"What?"

"You've had several wrong numbers recently?"

"Yes."

"We traced them. All from a couple of numbers, one of which we can connect to Toller. The device on your car would have been set off via a phone call, but we had already removed it."

"Oh God, they really mean this! I can accept the risks for me, but not for my family. I need to get the girls protected, and the boys and their families."

"It's already done. They're all safe, I assure you."

"Thank you. Now what?"

"We wait."

"How long have you known all was not right?"

"Not long. It was Jake alerted me to something. You know he keeps in touch with the travellers?"

"Yes, horse doctoring."

"Well, they told him Mabel was up to something. She has rallied her considerable family around her and broken off from the main group. There have been some high-powered travellers' meetings. He was told that they have decided Caleb is better off dead."

"So why take me out too? Could that not be done in prison?"

"He would happily come out into the open as it were if he thought he could take you out."

"Oh, I see."

Meanwhile, in the other room, Anna put the plate of sandwiches down on the coffee table, picked up her knitting and said,

"Are you frightened, Sharon?"

"Does it seem very cowardly to admit it? Yes, I am, as much for your husband as for me. I'm so sorry I brought all this on you."

"No, dear, you didn't. Being a policeman's wife has always had its risks. I must admit to being scared too, but we're safe here. Relax, have a coffee and a butty. It could be a long night. Now, tell me, how things have been going on the squad?"

"I've really enjoyed it. I've learned so much. The rest of the squad have been so helpful, Julia especially. I have been given most of the simpler jobs, but some of what I've done has turned up some good evidence."

"Have you made any friends?"

"Julia for certain and Tarik, he's great fun, and Caroline too. Sergeant Bickerstaff has been almost fatherly, he is my direct supervisor. He tells me what to look for, how to record it, and then checks my paperwork and points out any improvements; he's really kind."

"Yes, I do like Geoff. He and his wife went through a bad time when there was a murder at the Operatic Society. My daughter Susan is a junior member now."

"Yes, he told me. I prefer him to the other skipper Paul. They're all nice, but Geoff is the best."

"What's wrong with Paul?"

"Nothing I can put my finger on. He *is* helpful and said if I needed to talk, he was always there, and he is very friendly, but he asked me where I was living the other day. I came back in the office while Julia was parking the car and writing up the logbook. I came in with the statements we had taken. Paul was coming out of Mr Catchpole's office. He looked a bit startled and asked me where I was living, as he had been revising the details in case of a major callout. I told him I was living at the single officers' quarters on Darlington Street, at number 23. I happen to know that it was recently vacated. Then he asked me if I had somewhere to go if I was worried, as he knew the boss was concerned for my safety. I told him I would go to my parents, up in Cleveland. I'm not sure why I didn't trust him, but it just seemed wrong."

"Have you told Saul this?"

"No. I haven't had time. To be honest, I forgot. I haven't seen Paul since that evening."

"Then I think we must tell Saul now. Tell me, dear, who else don't you like?"

"Obviously, I like some more than others. There is one chap, Sean Hawkins, he never works with any of the women and goes out with Paul a lot. I asked Julia why, she said he's terrified of women and he is utterly ruled by his mother. I happen to know his mother is dead. The first sudden death I went to, when I joined the job, with my tutor, was his mother. He does not remember me and I have no wish to remind him. To be frank, he rather gives me the creeps."

"Anyone else?"

"Only one, but he interests me more than anything. Kevin Malpas. He's so quiet you can hardly get a word out of him. He's not shy as such, just rather withdrawn. He has the strangest eyes. They are such a pale grey they are almost white. I did an enquiry with him, talking to a witness. He was very good; we got a great statement. I asked Julia and she laughed and said that whatever he did was always as perfect as it could be. She says he is very bright and very observant and can read people very well."

"Is he married?"

"I don't think so. He's about thirty, skinny, ash blond hair, big ears, and as I said, very unusual eyes. All I know about him is that he was a teacher, he is left-handed, and he is a lactose intolerant. He has special milk for his tea or coffee. He has very elegant hands, pale, beautifully kept and as smooth as a baby's bum.

He grows alpine plants and enjoys bird watching. That's all I know."

"Rather a lot when you add it up. Here's Saul now. Sandwich, darling? Sharon and I have been chatting and we need to tell you some things."

Diana looked in on them about half an hour later.

"It looks like things are hotting up. They've found the laundry van."

Saul said, "And the driver?"

"Yes, he's pretty poorly. He has been rushed to intensive care. We think they then stole a car nearby. That has been found two villages from here. So, if you please, will you all go down to the cellars? There's a warm fire. Everything is there All the dogs are there, and your cat, Sharon."

Saul said, "Yes, you two go down, I'm staying up here."

In the cellar they settled down with the animals, Mung realizing that Sharon's lap was the perfect place to be. Sharon asked Anna if she had any spare knitting needles and wool and declared that she wished to learn to knit.

Back in the hall, Diana said, "I knew you would refuse to take cover, you impossible man! They're half a mile down the lane heading this way. We can do this one of two ways. Either we wait and see what they do, or we can lure them down to the river gorge, where they will be like fish in a barrel; but that has its risks. I was going to do that any way. It's all set up there."

"They're not looking to kill you, but me. I'll act as bait for you."

"We'll do it together. I know every inch down there which you do not. Stick with me like glue, please."

"All right, I agree. Diana, why do you need to put yourself at risk?"

"Because I'm good at it. If you don't do it my way, we wait here."

Having checked they had all the bullet proof clothing on correctly, fifteen minutes later they left the farmhouse and walked slowly down towards the river. Diana had explained that Jake was out of sight with the waiting armed unit. Saul felt the sweat pouring down the back of his neck. They had been talking softly to each other, as if on an evening stroll.

"How on earth do you keep so calm?"

"I only pretend. Don't look now, but over on the right someone is moving behind that hedge. Any minute now they'll fall into the old sheep dip trough. Yes, there they go. Now look startled and hurry with me down the gorge. Keep just ahead of me, now run!"

As they ran, they heard noises behind them over on their right, as they were pursued down the winding path which led to a small rocky area by the river.

Diana whispered, "Keep as low as you can. Head behind the big rock and into the cave entrance behind the big ash tree.

Several shots rang out behind them and Saul heard a thudding noise from where Diana was.

"Keep going you fool. No harm done. Run downstream behind that large tree."

Together they sheltered behind a massive willow tree. He said, "Are you hurt?"

"Not really, body armour is most effective. Here they come, into the ravine, from both directions. They think they have us trapped. Keep down and wait. Look to your right, can you see the cave entrance? Don't move yet."

"Why not?"

"We might learn something. Draw your gun and take the safety catch off. Be ready to fire."

"I take it you have one?"

"I do. Now call out to them, ask them who they are."

"To draw them in a bit closer?"

"Yes."

Saul raised his voice and called out, "Who are you, what are you doing here?"

"I am your nemesis, arsehole. I warned you. Not so brave now, are you?"

"Gilchrist, have you gone quite mad? This is not the way to improve things for you. You may kill me, but you will never get away with it."

"You may get me, but I don't care. I have nothing left to lose, but you have."

"Then call the others off, then I'll come out and face you."

"Not likely. Caleb, you there?"

226

"Yes, I'm here. I'll get him! Let me! He can't go nowhere. I'm going to enjoy this!"

"Okay, you take first shot."

Diana pulled Saul down and pushed him into the cave entrance which was not easily accessible from any distance. He crawled into the blackness and she said, "Keep going up the passage. I'll catch up. Quick, I'll cover you."

He moved into the passage. He heard a flurry of shots from outside the cave. Then he heard a loudspeaker and the sound of a helicopter overhead. There was a prolonged exchange of shots, a pause and then another exchange of shots. Then Diana turned and came into the passage and ran towards him. They had not gone far when she paused and said, "Shelter behind this bend here."

"What happened?"

"Gilchrist and Caleb won't worry you anymore. The others have either surrendered or are being picked up by the paramedics now. I think one got away, so we must wait and see if he makes it in here. Here give me your gun, and then reload mine for me."

"Why?"

"Because I'm the better shot."

They listened and waited. Saul suddenly heard a slight shuffling sound and then a figure came round the bend and into sight

He saw a glint of metal in the person's hand.

"Stay exactly where you are, throw the gun down where I can see it. I am an armed police officer and will fire, if you don't do as I tell you."

"I know who you are, Saul. You see, I've nothing to lose either. "I am sorry, I really liked and respected you, but you would have protected these animals and let them live. I couldn't do that. They deserved to die. It was the only way to get at them, to get that monster out, so we could finish his miserable existence. Whoever it is with you did the world a favour. You would only have put him back inside again."

"Paul? Now he's dead, give up. I can try to help you. Whatever happened, caused you to flip like this? Talk to me Paul. This will not be solved by violence. Give up and I promise I'll listen."

"No. I'll tell you now. I thought I could cope, do my job. I started interviewing these monsters who paid for the tapes. They got bail and fancy, clever, solicitors, mostly on legal aid that you and I pay for. They made excuses. Did not see, some of them, what they did wrong. The suffering and lives of the children meant nothing to them. All they wanted was a kick, a thrill to satisfy their lust. Yes, we might have put them away, but for how long? You would have done your job and then protected them. You fool! They would have got away with it. Do you know what that kind of abuse does to a kid? Have you any idea?"

"Not personally, no. I can't, as I've never experienced it. All I can do is rely on the law and get them put away."

"At least you admit you cannot know how it feels. I do know. It happened to me when I was a kid, for years. It was my uncle. I've tried to put it behind me; succeeded for a while. Then this brought it all flooding back. It just welled up like a big blackness. I knew then what I must do. I'm sorry Saul, but I cannot live with this, not with letting those bastards live. My uncle, you will find his body in the boot of his car, in his garage, at his cottage in the village of Cutsyke, Pasture Way. House called Fair View. He called it that because he could watch the little boys in the school from there. I was going to get Caleb next, but your lot have saved me the trouble. Then I was going to take out the worst ones on that list, but you obviously are a step or two ahead of us. And now I won't be able to."

"No, Paul, you won't. Think of your family, they need you."

"They will be better off without me. Do me a favour, friend, shoot me, will you? That way it won't be suicide and they'll get the insurance. If you won't, I'll do it myself."

"Why not let me help you instead, get you treatment, rehabilitation?"

"Always so damn reasonable, aren't you? I tell you I murdered my uncle and you want to help me. Well, you can't. It has all come back like a vivid nightmare. It won't go away. I cannot live with it. Thanks for trying, though."

"Did you want to kill me?"

"No. I wanted to kill Caleb. He wanted to kill you. To get him I had to use that. I couldn't even kill him, one of your lot did."

"Give up, please, Paul. I don't want to see you killed."

"If I fire at you, you will have to take me out. It's my only option now. My mind is coming apart. I can't live with what I've done, and with what I have not done. I've decided. I'm going to walk forward and shoot, and if you're in the way then at least I know you won't be helping any of these wicked men survive any more."

Paul raised the gun in his hand and pointed it at Saul, who said, "Paul, please, don't do this. I can help you and I will."

Paul fired several times and as he did so Saul dropped to the ground. The sound in the small passageway was thunderous. Saul watched as Paul dropped the gun and fell forwards with a neat hole between his eyes. That at least one bullet had hit the passage wall behind Saul, was evident as there were pieces of rock showering around him. The noise echoed around for what seemed like an eternity, but it was only a few seconds.

Diana said, "Are you hurt?"

"I don't think so. Did you have to kill him?"

"I did. I've done him the favour you couldn't. Don't touch him, stay on the ground. Here come the others."

Saul waited until he was ushered out by Mr Owen. He sat on a rock and watched as the carnage outside was being recorded. Owen sat beside him and confirmed, "It was all recorded. There was nothing more you could do. You did try."

"He was a friend. I should have seen how he was breaking up. I didn't. I failed him."

Diana, who had sat down beside them, was a little tougher on Saul when she spoke,

"Stop wallowing in self-recrimination. We all know he had flipped and was as mad as a hatter. I have what you tried to do, reasoning with him, recorded. Snap out of it and get back to the farmhouse."

"I suppose you're right. I wonder if everyone needs to know all his torment."

"Some of it, maybe. Until this, he was a fine man and officer. We can give his family that."

Saul walked back with Mr Owen and Diana out of the ravine and found the firearms team. An inspector came up to him and asked for his firearm.

Saul handed him the gun saying, "Paul Christie is dead."

"Yes, I know. You look very shaken up, get back to the house please."

"Do you not need me here?"

"Only if you can identify some of the bodies."

"How many?"

"Four. The rest are on their way to hospital, under arrest."

Saul, wrapped in a blanket that someone had put round him, looked at the bodies in front of him.

"That is Caleb Jones. The one over there is Anthony Gilchrist."

He walked over to another area and said, "This here is Toller. The other one I don't know, but I think may be a traveller. Are any police officers hurt?"

"Two, neither seriously."

They all returned to the main farmhouse, where Saul gave a statement to one of the investigating officers. He found Sharon and Anna in the sitting room. Jake joined them.

Saul said to Sharon, "I'm so sorry. Tony is dead. Have you been told?"

"I have, sir, and thank you. I'll cry no tears for him. It was his choice to do what he did. I'm sorry about Paul."

"I will have to tell his family."

"No, you won't," said Owen." "It's being done by Bickerstaff. Now listen Saul, Sharon, you're both now placed on leave for at least a fortnight. I will need to know where you are in case I need to contact you."

Anna said, "I can tell you now, Saul and I will be going up to Skye for a couple of weeks. We'll leave tomorrow. The girls can join us for the second week as it's their half term. I'll ring the hotel at Uig now. Is that all right?"

"Perfect. Look after him, please, Anna, he's a bit shaken up, quite understandably. Someone will pick you both up in about an hour and take you home."

When they got to their home, Anna went upstairs and had a shower. When she came down Saul said, "Skye? I thought you found it depressing when we were there last?"

"Not Skye itself, just the weather. You don't; I think it calms you. It's not your fault, darling. I just want to help."

Chapter 16

Alan Withers was hectically busy. Even with new office staff and help, he was struggling to keep abreast of the matters needing his attention. His admiration for Saul knew no bounds. Stepping into his shoes had been an enlightenment. He soon understood how much there was to do, not just heading an enquiry – that was within his experience – but the administration and personnel matters, and the press conferences. He had seen Saul briefly at Paul's funeral and at the inquests, but had found him almost distant and withdrawn, and very quiet. Alan went to the force welfare officer about it.

"I need your help. Not just for me, but for Mr Catchpole. The man I saw at the inquest was not the man I know. He is grey and he has lost quite a bit of weight. I spoke to his wife. She said he has gone somewhere in his mind. She cannot get through to him either. Can you help him?"

"His wife has already asked us to. They're due back at their home tomorrow. The chief is going out to see him soon, and his wife and his brother and sister-in-law, to offer counselling."

"I think I could do with some help too. I worked with Paul a lot and I never saw it. I feel guilty too."

"I was going to come into the squad offices this afternoon, to offer help, advice and counselling to any who feel the need."

"To be honest, I am worried Saul will resign over this."

"He has already tried, three times, and each time he has been told it will not be accepted. I think it might help if he felt he was needed."

"He is, I can't cope. I admit it. He did so much that I never saw. I will ask him."

"Do you know of anyone outside his family who he could totally confide in?"

"Actually, there is, his old boss, Duffy. I'll go and see him and explain. I know Saul will listen to him."

Two weeks later, Saul went back to work. There was a subdued murmur as he let himself into his office. They waited in silence until they heard an outraged bellow, followed by roars of laughter, and Saul stormed out of his office, with a bound volume in one hand, and wrapping paper in the other.

"Right, you lot of reprobates! I know I said I didn't want cartoons of animals. an almost verbatim transcript of my losing my temper. or the jokes that went with it on the walls, but I didn't mean you had to get them printed and bound. Just how many copies are there?"

The grin and the twinkle in his eyes made everyone relax.

"Geoff, Paddy, explain please?"

"Yes, sir, obviously your copy, the chief's copy, the office copy, and most of us have one, not to mention the one in the force library, Mr Owen and your sister-in-law..."

"Who else?"

"One or two. Welcome back, sir, we have missed you."

"Well I'm here now."

"There is something else before you're told by anyone else."

"What?

"We decided to have a memorial plaque for Paul, in the chapel. Do you mind?"

"Not at all. Why not one in here as well?"

"We can?"

"Of course. I need to talk to everyone about what happened, call a meeting sometime today."

Later, at the meeting, Saul told his squad what had happened in the cave. He glossed over the danger he had been in and Paul's attempt to shoot him, but several of the squad had already been told.

Tarik said, "He did help Gilchrist and Caleb escape. I enquired at the prison and they told me they had expressed their concerns to Paul Christie when he went to do follow up interviews with them. This was, incidentally, when he was officially on leave. When Sharon saw him that evening here in your office, he was on leave. I checked back and found that on that evening, one of the squad cars was out, but there was no record in the logbook. I had been trying to find who had driven it. Then I ran into a mate of mine downstairs and he told me he had seen Paul in it one evening, he just assumed he was on duty. The mileage unaccounted for was to the prison and back. The prison confirmed that he had been there. They have a list of our vehicles and would have queried a private car. As I think most of you know, the laundry van driver has come off the danger list. He will, hopefully, make a full recovery.

Alan went on to explain that the body of Paul's uncle had been found where he said it was, with a huge amount of child pornography, some connected to the cases being dealt with, in his house. A neighbour had confirmed he had seen Paul, which they thought unusual, on the day the uncle must have been killed. He then said, "What I don't know is what happened to Sean Hopkins. Do you know, sir?"

"Yes, I do. He has resigned, because he was caught out trying to conceal evidence of pornography implicating an uncle of his living down south. The chief has accepted the resignation and thinks that will suffice in his case. The other thing I think you should know is that Kevin Malpas and Sharon Wright will shortly be leaving us. They're being posted to another department, to their credit."

Geoff said, "There is also a matter that needs to be sorted. As you know, Caroline and Alan get hitched this weekend, and will be away on honeymoon, but on Saturday, most of us are coming to the wedding, so we need someone to cover the office that day, for any calls and anything urgent."

"I'll come in with Mario that day, if you like."

"Thank you, DC Hart and DC Verdi. That would be ideal. I am sure someone will bring you some cake!"

The wedding was happy occasion. The squad had clubbed together and gave Alan and Caroline some lovely gifts for their new home.

On the Sunday, Saul and Anna went to the farm to spend the day with Jake and Diana. After a substantial lunch, Jake and Anna went and dozed in the sitting room, and Diana and Saul went for a walk with the dogs.

"Di, thanks for everything you did. I know I owe you my life. You were right."

"I hope I was. You know your main problem? You care far too much. You're far too good for what you do. I wasn't emotionally involved, which is why I could do what I did. My main objective was to keep you alive."

"I know, but I've got a few questions."

"Of course you have. Fire away."

"How do you know you're a better shot than me?"

"I don't, but I expect I am. At the time I had to keep both our minds focused. Are you a particularly good shot?"

"Not really, I'm a little above average, nothing special."

"Well, I'm a top marksman, have been for years. I wasn't trying to be arrogant."

"Good. I know you thought Sharon was good, but what made you decide she was clever enough to do your kind of work?"

"When she beat me at chess, not once, but several times. She sees things and has the ability to think ahead. She noticed things about Kevin too, and Anna told me. I had a look at him and probed a bit."

"I always thought him rather introverted."

"He is, but he has talent. His major asset is also his major weakness. He is very, very clever, but he tries to hide it. He is very shy. I met him and had a long talk with him."

"I thought for your kind of work you had to be unremarkable. He's quite distinctive with those eyes,"

"Not a problem in his case. I think he will do very well. They both will."

"Who are you going to pinch from me next? I don't want to lose too many officers."

"I need to talk to you about that at some time, not urgent but there is someone else I need."

"Who?"

"You, in due course. When you leave the force."

"How long have you been lining me up for it?"

"Since we first met, many years ago. Think about it and talk it over with Anna."

"Why with her?"

"Because she's already on the team, since she retired from teaching."

"Why did she not tell me?"

"Because I asked her not to."

"You devious, sly dog!"

"We're not going back to animal impressions, are we?"

"Bitch! That was below the belt. You should have told me. I had a right to know."

"Did you? Do I detect a male chauvinist 'I'm head of my family and in control of them' attitude here? I thought you were more liberal than that. Is Anna not a person in her own right?"

"Certainly she is, and yes, you're right, I'm being quite unfair. If Anna wishes to do it, I have no grounds for standing in her way. I just want her safe, that's all."

"Which she will be. I just want her problem-solving ability, not field work, from both of you."

"Fair enough. I am sorry I called you a bitch."

"I'm not. I can now call you names if I want to. I cannot think of many right now, just give me time. I don't have your animal vocabulary."

"I asked for that."

"True!"

"I'll probably forgive you."

"Until it is to your advantage to remember it. I'll get my own back in time. You might want to, but you're too gentle. Now shall we accept that I'm devious, you're pig headed, my husband is a big soft bear, and that Anna is brighter than all of us? Let's talk about something else."

"What?"

"You did some painting up in Skye?"

"Yes quite a few, why?"

"You did one up on the Quiraing. Can I buy it, please?"

"No, you can have it, but why that one?"

"It was there I lost my first husband. I think maybe we should wash the dogs in the river before taking them back."

"I think you're right. What else will you be shocking me with?"

"Only one thing. Sharon Wright and Kevin Malpas might well become an item. They're very attracted to each other but don't know how much yet."

"Are they?"

"If it happens, I can use them as a team."

"You amaze me. How do you know these things?"

"I'm a woman, we just do. Anna told me. I think it's almost time for tea."

"I shall never understand women."

"Men are not meant to. If they did, the world would fall apart."

"Can women understand men?"

"Of course they can. Men are sad, simple beings, transparent, solid and utterly predictable, most of the time. That makes it so difficult when they change for some reason."

"That went over my head."

"I expect it did. Never mind."

"I'm not sad!"

"No, not anymore. You were, but I think you're healed now."

"You devious, manipulative shrew!"

"I'll have to put that on the list. You know I have a copy of the book?"

"Yes, it really cheered me up when I saw just how it had been used to cheer everyone else up. I was a little taken aback when I saw it was entitled *'On the road to Damascus!'*"

"I thought it was rather apt."

"You probably suggested it, did you?"

"I might have done."

As Saul was driving home that evening, he looked over at Anna who was smiling to herself

"What's so funny?"

"Nothing, dear, I'm just happy."

"What about?"

"You, darling. You are back to my wonderful, brave husband. Wherever it is you went in your mind, is far behind you now. There were vestiges of it this morning, but they're gone. Did talking to Diana help?"

"Yes, it did. She explained a lot; not obviously, that's not her way, as you know. She subtly plants suggestions and leaves me to work it out. You're right, I am healed. I can look forward now, I couldn't before."

"I know. So can I. Can I tell you something?"

"About you working for her, I know."

"Not that, it is about her. I think talking to you has helped her. Jake had a long chat with me. She's not as tough as she makes out."

"Really?

"She's been down since that gun fight in the cave. Jake says she has been having nightmares. I know Diana, probably better than you do. She hates killing anything. She's been racked with remorse."

"Why didn't she say?"

"Because to heal your guilt she had to hide hers. I think healing first me, then you, has healed her. Now, let's get home. I love you Saul, very much"

"And I love you, Anna."

"I know dear, I always have."

The End